ELI THE GOOD

ELI THE GOOD

= SILAS HOUSE =

CANDLEWICK PRESS

Fic
Hou

Copyright © 2009 by Silas House

"Trees" from *Flower & Hand* by W. S. Merwin. Copyright © 1997 by W. S. Merwin, reprinted with permission of The Wylie Agency LLC.

First edition 2009

Library of Congress Cataloging-in-Publication Data

House, Silas, date.
Eli the Good / Silas House. — 1st ed.
p. cm.
Summary: In Kentucky in the summer 1976, ten-year-old Eli Book's excitement over Bicentennial celebrations is tempered by his father's flashbacks to the Vietnam War and other family problems, as well as concern about his tough but troubled best friend, Edie.
ISBN 978-0-7636-4341-6
[1. Family problems — Fiction. 2. Post-traumatic stress disorder — Fiction. 3. Best friends — Fiction. 4. Friendship — Fiction. 5. American Revolution Bicentennial, 1976 — Fiction. 6. Aunts — Fiction.]
I. Title.
PZ7.H81558Eli 2009
[Fic] — dc22   2009004589

09 10 11 12 13 14 BVG 10 9 8 7 6 5 4 3

Printed in Berryville, VA, U.S.A.

This book was typeset in Granjon.

Candlewick Press
99 Dover Street
Somerville, Massachusetts 02144

visit us at www.candlewick.com

For my father

PART ONE

June

The summer that I was ten —
Can it be there was only one
summer that I was ten? It must
have been a long one then —

—May Swenson, "The Centaur"

ONE

That was the summer of the bicentennial, when all these things happened: my sister, Josie, began to hate our country and slapped my mother's face; my wild aunt, Nell, moved in with us, bringing along all five thousand or so of her records and a green record player that ran on batteries; my father started going back to Vietnam in his dreams, and I saw him cry; my mother did the Twist in front of the whole town and nearly lost us all. I was ten years old, and I did something unforgivable.

The first true day of summer for me began with a scream. Only one long, choked, jagged cry, but the sound was full of so much terror that I jumped out of a deep sleep, straight from the bed and onto the cool floorboards. By the time I was on my feet, morning stillness had overtaken the house again, but then I could hear people moving about and I unfroze myself so I could venture out into the hallway.

My sister, Josie, was standing in the doorway of her room, looking down the hall toward my parents' bedroom, as if expecting some other sound to give us direction as to what we should do. But all we heard was my mother cooing our father's name.

"Stanton, it's okay," she whispered, like wind in big leaves. Then, his whole name, as if to remind him who he was: "Stanton Book. Stanton."

Josie, who was sixteen and nice to no one except me, put her hand out and I took it. We moved down the hallway with caution, stepping through squares of white sunlight that fell on the floor. She kept hold of my hand but also walked just behind me, her other hand on the back of my neck, as if steering me.

Their door was ajar, so Josie called out, "Loretta? Stanton?" She had taken to calling our parents by their first names that summer, much to their dismay.

"It's all right," my mother said, but Josie brought up her toe and pushed the door aside anyway. Only a crack, but enough that I could see in. Daddy was sitting on the edge of the bed with his feet on the floor, and Mom was on her knees in the bed, her hands on his back. Daddy didn't turn to look at us, but the morning light was falling onto his face so that it shone out to us. His eyes looked far away, like he might not know we were all there.

Mom peered at us as if we were witnessing something we shouldn't. Her eyes were full of a kind of fright I couldn't name at that moment, but later I realized that it was a sort of new knowledge there on her face. Maybe for the first time she knew exactly what the war had done to her husband. "Go on, now," she whispered, nodding. "He's just dreamed of Vietnam. That's all. Everything's all right."

I kept staring at my father, though. He was rocking on the edge of the bed now, his hands up to his face. The muscles at the top of his back were stretched tight. I hated the fact that I barely knew him. He was most often good to me, sometimes snatching me up to ride me on his shoulders, tousling my hair, even letting me sit in his lap and drive his truck up the road every once in a while. Then there were times when his temper flared for no known reason, so that we always felt like we were walking through a minefield, waiting for an explosion.

Once I had asked him to tell me about the war and his only response had been a tightening of his jaw before he said, "No. Never," and then walked away without looking back. My mother had felt no pity for me in this moment. "Drop it," she'd said, in her I'm-not-budging voice. But most of all he was just quiet, a man who lived in the shadows of his family. That was the hardest part, and it left me a boy surrounded by all these women, all the time. Not a bad thing, but sometimes it was confusing and lonesome.

"Josie," Mom hissed, and nodded to me, so that Josie grabbed hold of my hand again and we moved away with hesitation, even walking backward for a few steps. Finally Josie directed me back down the hallway, dropping my hand at her bedroom door so she could yawn with balled-up fists going into the air. Her oversize Led Zeppelin shirt rode up too high and showed her panties.

"Now that I've been scared to death properly," Josie said, "I believe I'll go back to bed for a little while."

Daddy had been awaking us all with his screams lately, so once Josie knew that it was another Vietnam dream, she saw no reason to be upset. I suppose she thought she was used to living with screaming and war, but I had not been able to convince myself of this yet. There was no way I would be able to go back to sleep, and my nerves would be on edge the rest of the day. I worried a lot about Daddy. I worried about everything. I worried about the Russians dropping a nuclear bomb on us. About Josie talking mean to our mother. I worried that Daddy would snap one day and let his anger go too far and hurt one of us.

"Well, go on," Josie said, nudging me toward my room while she ground a fist into her eye. "Get back in the bed. It's not even seven o'clock yet, and it's *summer*."

"I'm going riding," I announced.

Josie nodded. She would have agreed to anything if it meant she could go back to sleep. She ran a hand through her hair and stumbled into her room. "Be careful, little man," she said, and eased her door shut.

I pulled on a pair of blue-jean cutoffs and a muscle shirt. Chuck Taylor shoes with no socks. Last I put on my Uncle Sam hat, which we had made on the last day of school. Mine had turned out especially good, so I wore it every day when I went riding on my bicycle. I ran on out and found my bike where I had left it, a layer of cool dew standing on my seat.

It was only six thirty, but the world was wide awake like me, and white with summer light. The air was still cool with morning, and even though it held the heat of yesterday beneath, there were goose bumps all down the underside of my arm. The trees behind our house were filled with bird-call. I straddled my bike and stood listening, watching the trees for a sign of the birds. My mother could name every bird by its song, but I had never been able to do this.

I had brought along my transistor radio, so I latched it to the handlebars. There was nothing on yet except for the tobacco reports, so I snapped the radio back off and tried to figure out where to go. Before I had a chance to jump on, I heard someone calling my name.

It was Edie. She was my best friend, but I never would have admitted this to anyone back then. If I had let it be known that a girl was my best friend, the boys never would have let me live it down.

She was in her backyard, which bordered ours, leaning against the big old willow she loved. Her father was always threatening to cut it down, saying its leaves made too much of a mess in the fall. So far Edie had been able to talk him out of it. She was crazy over that willow tree.

"You coming or not?" she said, since I was standing there, looking at her. She didn't have to raise her voice, as it carried well on the morning air. "Or are you just going to stare at me like a retard?"

I walked my bicycle across our backyards and put the kickstand down — I couldn't stand kids who let their bikes fall to the ground — and squatted next to her. "What're you doing up so early?" I asked.

She shrugged. "I just woke up, wide awake. I think the birds woke me up. Listen at 'em." She put her forehead against the tree. "What about you?"

"Daddy woke us all up early. He had another bad nightmare, about the war."

She sat up straighter, interested. "What'd he do?"

"He just hollered out. But it scared us all to death."

"Does he ever talk to you, about the war?"

"No. Not about being over there."

"You ought to ask him about it."

"Why?"

"I don't know," she said, but she looked at me as if I

were stupid. "It'd be interesting, that's all. Don't you think it would?"

"Yeah. But he wouldn't tell me nothing."

"You never know until you try." This was one of Edie's mottoes. She believed in trying everything, in not being afraid of new things. She believed in not judging other people based on how they looked and in having what she called "an open mind." She was eighteen months older than me, but we had been friends before either of us could remember, so it didn't matter that she was older. She hung around with all of us boys because there were no girls on our road. I don't believe Edie would have played with girls even if there had been some, though. She was as good as a boy, anyway, and all of us knew this, even if we never would have admitted it aloud. She was tough. She could balance herself as she walked across the narrowest fallen tree, carry more rocks to build the dam than anyone else, climb the steepest cliff without shedding a tear if her legs got all scratched up from the rocks. All of us boys lived in secret fear of her, to be honest. We all knew that she could beat us at most things. It was bad enough to lose at something, but to be beaten by a girl was the ultimate humiliation. Once, Paul Shepherd had tried to put his hand down Edie's shorts and she had hit him in the face with her fist and called him a Communist pervert. He ran away crying, blood streaming out of his nose, and Edie just laughed.

"Run to Mommy, little wussy!" she called after him,

then turned to the rest of us, who stood nearby, mesmerized. "That's what he gets for messing with me."

Lately, though, Edie had started looking more like a girl. I hadn't really noticed, but Matt Patterson, who lived four houses down the road, had been riding bikes with me only a week earlier when he had asked if I had seen Edie's boobs.

"Boobs?" I said. "What do you mean?"

"You know, stupid," he said, and put on his brakes, causing the back wheel of his bike to take a crooked, sliding halt in the dirt. I stopped next to him and watched as he used his thumbs and forefingers to make two little tents at the top of his shirt, pulling them out. "Like *Laverne and Shirley*."

"No, she don't," I'd said, and took off, pedaling hard so that it took him a while to catch up with me.

Edie lay back against the tree, tucked into an indentation of the trunk that seemed to fit her perfectly.

"I've been getting up every morning and sitting against the tree," she said, with her eyes closed. "It has a good soul."

"You're crazy, man," I said, although I didn't believe this. Lately I had started putting *man* on the end of my sentences, the way Josie did.

She stood on her knees, the way my mother had been doing in the bed, comforting Daddy. She grabbed my wrist. "Here, put your hand on it." I let her direct me to the trunk of the willow. I noticed that she had on white fingernail polish. I had never seen her wear any kind of makeup before. I laid my palm flat against the tree and was surprised by the cool bark. "Now just be quiet, and listen."

We sat there in silence for a time. I watched her face, waiting for her to tell me more. "Close your eyes, and feel," she said.

I did. I shut my eyes and listened to the birds. Her hand remained on my wrist for what seemed a long while, but she eased it away. Then the birdcall faded and there was a big silence that made me notice only the sensation in my palm, where my skin was tingling from contact with the old willow.

"You feel it, don't you?" she whispered. "The trees, they can talk to you if you listen hard enough."

I was listening hard.

Often, when I met someone for the first time, I could tell if they were a good person or not. I just *knew*. And that's the way I felt in that moment, like the tree was good, too, and that I knew it without knowing why.

Lately I had realized that I was different from most other people, and I still wasn't sure how I felt about that. I had begun to think that I might be a writer. I definitely read more than normal kids. I read and wrote all the time. That year alone I had already read *Sounder, Where the Lilies Bloom* (my favorite), two Louis L'Amour westerns, *Where the Red Fern Grows,* and *The Light in the Forest.*

My idol was John-Boy Walton, and I had started saving every dime I could scrape up to buy myself a little typewriter like the one he had on *The Waltons*. Meanwhile, stories popped into my head and I scribbled them into my black-and-white composition book.

I hadn't told anyone of this. I liked the idea of having this secret as my own, during a time when I felt nothing at all belonged to me. Being a writer was a fate I had accepted, although I was not as open to accepting that I was weird.

I was also a country boy. My father was very proud of us being country people, so I strived to please him in this regard. My greatest hope was to make Daddy proud of me, and I would have done anything to make this happen, but the fact was that I would have been a country boy regardless.

Suddenly there was a faint, building buzz in my hand, as if the tree was humming beneath my palm. The willow was sending me some kind of reassuring message. I was sure of it. The trees were a part of me.

I jerked my hand away, like someone who has gotten too close to a flame.

"You're weird," I said, not sure if I wanted her to know how weird I was, too. I rubbed my palms together, trying to rid myself of the sensation in my right hand.

"I like being weird," she said. She looked pleased with herself, smiling at me. Edie had very blue eyes, which is the thing everyone always remembered about her. "But you felt it. I know you did. I could see it in your face."

I stood, tapped my kickstand up with the side of my shoe, and hopped on my bike. "Come on, let's go riding."

We pedaled up the road and watched the world come awake. The houses along our road were almost identical: small, plain, all with a porch that ran the whole width of their fronts. Since everybody had pretty good jobs but no intentions to move, many of the families had built on an extra room or a screen porch. These additions only made the sameness of the houses more noticeable, though. The add-ons looked as if they had fallen out of the sky and attached themselves.

These homes had once been company housing. The women all tried to make them look different with paint and flowers, but they were all still just alike. Blue trim around the windows or doors painted red or forsythia bushes didn't change anything; all the houses were the same underneath.

One by one, each little house showed life. My mother's best friend, Stella, who lived three doors down, came out with a laundry basket propped on her hip. She let it fall at her feet and immediately began to pin sheets to the clothesline. Finley Hopkins fired up his truck and backed out, heading to work at the Altamont Mines. Old hateful Miss Lawson was sweeping her front porch in a great fury, swinging the broom back and forth as if the fate of the world might depend on the cleanliness of her porch.

On the other side of the road from the houses were the shoals of the Refuge River. The water was never more than six inches deep there during the summer. Teenage girls like Josie carried lawn chairs on up the river, past the big cliffs where the kids weren't allowed, to lie in the sun. There they lay back with their fingers occasionally scooping up water to splash out over their naked bellies. They talked about Leif Garrett and listened to ABBA and Steve Miller on a transistor radio. Farther up the river was a big biscuit-shaped rock that hung out over a deep swimming hole where the water was suddenly still. I was too young to remember, but Josie claimed that when she was about ten we had lived through the hottest summer in history. She said the heat had been so bad that everybody on our road had come together at the swimming hole on one ungodly hot July day. Even the old people. "You never seen so much white flesh in your life," Josie said. "God, it was horrible." But something in her face told me it had been nice some-how, too.

Soon we were past all the houses and up where the woods took over one side of the road and the river widened on the other side. Stripes of mist moved down the hillsides and burned away in the new morning. We raced. We each rode a stretch without holding our handlebars, a trick Edie had taught me.

After a while we turned around and headed back the way we had come. I clicked on the radio and the deejay was encouraging everyone to stock up on fireworks for the bicentennial celebration on July Fourth. Then he gave the weather and said it was going to be the hottest day of the year so far. "I'm going to play a big hit from the summer of '74 to get you all up and moving this morning," he said, and then "I Can Help" came on. Josie had this record and still played it all the time. We pedaled in rhythm to the song, let our bicycles sway and veer across the road along with the weaving music. We both knew every word and sang it very loud. Stella heard the music as we coasted by and turned from her work at the clothesline to snap her fingers and dance a little. We laughed at that and kept singing. Everyone loved Stella.

When we rode back by my house, I realized that Daddy had already left for work at the station. I had wanted to tell him good-bye. When I noticed his truck was gone, I stopped in the middle of the road and stood with my legs on either side of my bike, watching the house as if he might magically reappear. Edie had sped on past me, but now she had noticed that I was stopped in the middle of the road, staring at the house like a dullard. She hollered and laughed at me but I couldn't move for a time, and eventually she rode away, putting her arms in the air to ride with no hands.

TWO

I ran up the path as dusk came in with purple and red and a kind of whiteness I cannot explain. The light was different that summer, a clean light that filtered through the leaves and made them look like pieces of typing paper that had been cut in the shape of leaves. When the sun went down, everything cooled instantly, leaving the world to smell like cooked greens.

I sat in my secret place: the roots of my beech tree, where I could look out over the valley, waiting for my mother to come onto the porch to call my name. This was the only time of day when I felt she actually knew I existed, when she stood there on the porch, holding on to the banister and calling for me, the pulsating air of the gloaming around her.

I waited, my chin resting on the tops of my knees. The sun was melting fast, spreading out along the horizon like butter. The breath of wind that had been stirring the leaves stopped. All birdcall ceased. Not one dog barked; no one hollered out as they ran across a yard. Everything became completely still as if the whole world realized this moment without knowing it. This hushed time of day carried its own scent, too, a low sweetness like honeysuckle that hadn't bloomed yet, like honeysuckle that didn't even know it was about to bloom. The sun sank lower and lower and then: "Eli!"

My mother's voice. If I had moved from my spot and crawled out onto the edge of the bluff, I could have seen her standing out on the back porch, her elbows in her hands as she scanned the yard. "Eli! It's time to come in now!"

I held my breath and felt like the whole world was waiting with me.

"Eli?" A question now. The shoals of the river were quiet; all the other kids had gone home. It was the same every day of summer. Now she would call out more firmly—"*Eli!*"—and then I would stand and take one final look at the sunset before running through the woods, down the old path, and into our backyard.

My mother didn't see me coming out of the trees. She walked to the corner of the screen porch, leaned against one of the posts, and called my name again, a long stretching of the two syllables of my name, turning "Eli" into a little song that I never tired of hearing.

It's important that you know this: my mother was beautiful. Everybody said so. She must have driven the boys at the high school absolutely crazy, pacing back and forth in front of the blackboard while she tried to teach them biology. Her hair was always just right, even though she didn't pay a bit of attention to it. Daddy always said she was one of those women who have a talent for pulling her hair up in a matter of seconds without a thought. Usually she pinned it up with a single barrette in the center of her scalp, showing off her broad, smart forehead. Her eyes were green and clever, alert to everything happening around her. At the same time, there was a distance about my mother that was most noticeable in her eyes. A mystery there kept everyone — even me, especially me — from getting too close, although we all wanted to be close to her more than anything, wanted to know everything about her.

She was only thirty-three years old that summer, and her beauty was in full bloom, a kind of peach tint that overtook her face and caused her to glow from within. People stopped talking when she dashed by on the street. There was something about the way she moved. She was set apart from the other women we knew because of the gracefulness she possessed. It was more than that, though. She was unusually confident, a strength that showed not only in her eyes but also in the determined steps she took in everyday motion. She always looked as if she had somewhere important to go.

"There you are," she said, her voice no more than three breaths, and the screen door cried open as she stepped down from the porch and onto the top step. She put her hand on my head as I leaned into her, my face against her waist. She smelled like lemon Joy, and I knew she had been washing dishes. For the rest of my life that scent has conjured up longing in me. "I's getting worried about you," she said.

"I was right there," I said, pointing to the ridge. "Watching you."

"It's just you and me tonight," she said, and opened the door to the screen porch. "Your daddy's going to be real late, and Josie is fixing to go to the drive-in with Charles Asher."

"Can I go with her?" As we stepped into the house, I could smell the dishwater and the coffee she always kept warming on the stove. She drank two pots a day, sometimes, even in the hottest part of summer. From the bathroom down the hall, I could hear the muffled sound of Josie's radio, playing Bob Seger.

"Nawsir, you cannot." Mom tipped a stream of coffee into a cup and leaned against the counter, taking a drink while she held one elbow in her free hand. "You have to stay here and keep me company."

"I'm going to watch Josie get ready," I said, heading down the hall.

"All right, then," she said. I looked back to see her smiling at me with her hooded eyes. Sometimes she looked at me like that, with a strange mix of amusement and love and puzzlement. There was a wall between my mother and me that I couldn't accept, even though I knew what it was: she loved my father more than me. This was hard for me.

Once I had spied on my parents watching Johnny Carson together when I was supposed to be in bed. They were lying all curled up together on the couch, one of Daddy's legs thrown over both of hers. My father realized about the same time as me that my mother was crying. He asked what was wrong, and she rolled over so he could run his thumb down the side of her face. She kissed his whole face, a dozen times on his eyes, his lips, his cheeks, his forehead. "I love you too much," she said, still crying. "More than anything. More than anybody."

I don't believe I ever completely forgave her for that.

Strangely enough, there was no distance at all between my sister, Josie, and me. Although she was six years my senior, we got along better than any other brother and sister I knew.

"Hey, little man," she said, looking at me by way of the mirror when I walked in. She never called me Eli, only this nickname she had given to me when I was a baby. She was leaned in to the mirror so close that her nose almost touched the glass. Her eyes were those of a lost girl. I didn't know it at the time, but she had recently had her entire history called into question, and this had marked her, had made her harder and stronger. I did know that she was searching for something that summer.

I pulled myself up onto the vanity counter and watched her. I loved the careful way she went about putting on her blue eye shadow, how she spent much more time and patience on this than on anything else. She mouthed the words to the song playing on the radio: *Beautiful loser, where you gonna fall?*

"Mom's going to *die,*" I said, and left my eyes on her pants so she'd know what I was talking about.

Josie had this pair of pants that was always causing trouble, and she had them on that evening. They looked like the American flag — each leg was striped in red and white, and above that was a blue block pecked with small white stars. Our mother hated these pants, which only added to Josie's love for them. In fact, whenever she wasn't wearing them, she hid the pants, afraid Mom would find them and throw them away. She had shared the hiding place's location with no one else but me, and I knew how much this meant, to be trusted in such a way. She only kept three things in the hiding place: the pack of cigarettes she sometimes smoked from, the pint of Jim Beam she had stolen from Stella's house, and the pair of flag pants that our mother hated.

"She'll get over it," Josie said. "If she don't, then tough."

"I hate it when you all fight," I said, but Josie didn't answer. She was putting on her lipstick, a frosty pink that was almost white. She didn't wear much makeup—only eye shadow and lipstick—but she and Mom fought over that, too. Mom said that when she was young, girls didn't wear makeup until they were grown. Josie's reply was always that she *was* grown. She ripped off three squares of toilet paper, folded them, blotted her lips, and handed them to me without glancing my way.

"Daddy's never said anything about them," she said. "And he's the one who was in the war. Not her."

I looked down at the perfect bloom of her lips for a time before I realized that stillness had seized her.

Josie was looking into the mirror as if transfixed. She sang one verse of the song—*beautiful loser, read it on the wall*—beneath her breath, concentrating on each word. There was a tight look of disgust on her face, a scowl that didn't really change the shape of anything. Still, she looked awfully cool to me, standing there in flag pants and what she called a peasant blouse and her black hair so long that she could sit on it. The top of her head shone in the light of the bare bulb hanging over the bathroom sink.

Josie stood there like one of the mannequins in the window of the Cato's downtown, staring without blinking. The drip of the faucet grew louder. Finally, she let out an exaggerated sigh. When she put a hand into her hair and lifted it, the clean green-apples smell of her shampoo washed out over me and caused my mouth to water.

Josie put a knuckle against my arm and let her eyes touch mine, her sign that she was finished. She took a step back as I slid from the counter, as if she didn't trust that I would be able to get down properly. When I was smaller, she had slid her hands under my arms and helped me down, but I wouldn't let her do this anymore.

Just as I hopped down, Mom appeared in the bathroom door, which I had left ajar. She had a talent for magically appearing as if out of thin air. She held a cup of coffee with a fist of steam rising from the surface.

"Josie, I told you plain and simple I didn't want to see those old pants again," she said.

Josie crossed her arms. "Why?" She leaned out with the one word. "What is the *big* deal?"

"Your daddy almost got killed fighting for this country," Mom said, just as she always did. She lived with Vietnam stamped across her face as much as our father did. "I won't have you out in public with the flag plastered across your hind end."

Josie kicked the door with her sandaled foot. "I hate you!" This was becoming a daily declaration in our house, and it always made my stomach hurt to hear such a thing spoken out loud. I couldn't imagine a worse thing for one person to say to another. There was a secret between them that I didn't know about yet. I hated seeing them into it like that. There were times when Mom drew her hand back, but let it quiver in the air, never striking Josie. Once Josie had sidled up as close as she could to Mom and screamed in her face. It was getting worse. I despised the way they looked at each other, the disappointment flattening their brows, their voices scratching up from way back in their throats.

Mom looked Josie in the eye, unfazed by her outburst. "March in there and pull the pants off and hand them to me," she said. "They're going in the fire barrel."

Josie took a step forward. "If you do that, I'll never speak to you again."

Mom took a slow drink of her coffee, and as she brought the cup down, she gave a crooked little grin. "The way you've been acting lately, that might not be such a bad thing."

Josie took one big step out of the bathroom and stomped down the hallway, trying to make her way to the back door. We followed on her heels, and just as Josie reached the kitchen, Mom caught her by the wrist. She pulled Josie in toward her, their eyes boring into each other. Mom spoke solidly, each word measured into the same amount of force: "You're not going out dressed like that."

"Watch me," Josie spat, her voice filled with a venom found only in an overdramatic actress. Mom sometimes said that Josie had watched too many bad Bette Davis movies on the late show. Still, defeat showed in Josie's eyes as she stood there in a staring standoff with our mother. At last she ripped her wrist from Mom's grasp and bolted back down the hall-way. She ran into her bedroom and slammed the door.

We stood there without moving or speaking until Josie came back out, dressed in a different, regular, pair of bell-bottoms. Mom stood with her arms folded as Josie passed by her, giving one final glare of defiance to our mother and running her hand over my head as she passed. There was no victory in Mom's face as she watched Josie walk out the back door, going to stand beside the road until Charles Asher came to get her in his beautiful 1966 Mustang, which I coveted.

THREE

The firecrackers started popping as soon as darkness grew thick. Everybody had started celebrating freedom a full month before the actual Fourth of July. As soon as school had gotten out at the end of May, the fireworks had started up every night. Bottle rockets fizzed up into the air, and Roman candles shot out spinning balls of fire. There were fireworks for sale at little shacks set up alongside the road. The men who worked at these stands never wore shirts, and sometimes their girlfriends sat there with them, fanning themselves with magazines and rolling their cold Dr Pepper bottles across their foreheads.

"Turn it up," my mother said, nodding to the television. "I can't hear on account of them old firecrackers."

My mother and I were having supper together, sitting cross-legged on the living-room floor and eating from metal TV trays straddling our laps while we watched *Happy Days*. This is something that Mom would have never ever done if Daddy and Josie had been home. We also would not have eaten something as simple as macaroni cooked in tomato juice, but it was my favorite meal, and I loved the way Mom kept salting hers and leaning over her bowl with her shoulders hunched up, eating steadily without taking her eyes off the television, which she hardly ever watched.

"Who's that?" she said.

"That's Potsie. He's Richie's best friend."

"What's that redheaded one's name?"

"That's Ralph Malph."

"Lord have mercy, what kinds of names do these people have?" She frowned at the screen. "Fonzie, Potsie, Ralph Malph. Real people don't have names like that."

As the show ended, I realized that the whole room had gotten dark as we ate in the blue glow of the television. There was something about that eerie tint to the room that made it feel close and comfortable, the way a warm quilt changes a winter's day. The windows were open, and I knew that people out on their porches could hear the voices on our TV. Normally we would've been out on the porch, too. In the summertime, we always ate supper and then everyone made their way onto our screen porch, my father's favorite place in the wide world. He announced this all the time. "We sure are lucky," he'd say, settling into his chair. "There's nowhere else I'd rather be than right here."

Mom set her tray on the floor when *Happy Days* was over. "Oh, my God, it's completely dark," she said, as if shocked. She leaned back against the couch, not looking much older than Josie to me. She studied me for a time, and at last a smile broke out on her face. "We ought to dance," she said.

She jumped up and clicked on the lamp, snapped off the television, and started going through her albums that stood in a metal stand beside the record player. Friends of Josie's were always saying how our parents were cool, since they listened to things that most other parents did not. My mother loved rock 'n' roll. When she was younger, she and my aunt Nell had been crazy about the Doors.

She flipped through the albums, ticking them off one by one. "Linda Ronstadt? Nah. Oh, here's Cat Stevens."

"We can't dance to him," I said. "Do we have 'Waterloo'?"

"Your sister would die if she found out we'd been dancing to ABBA," she said, keeping her eyes on the records. Josie sometimes went into long speeches about why ABBA was ruining music, but I still liked them anyway. Mom kept going through the albums until she held up one with a golden-faced man on the cover. "Here we go," she said, nodding. "Van Morrison."

Mom slid the album out of its jacket and held it between two flat palms as she put it on the record player. "You used to love this song when you were real little. I'd put you on my hip and dance all over the house."

She set the needle on the first groove: "Brown-Eyed Girl." As the guitar picked out the beginning, Mom started snapping her fingers and moving her shoulders up and down. She sashayed across the living room, took my hands, intertwining our fingers as she spun me around the room. The song built to its chorus of celebration, and then she let go and danced in front of me, her eyes closed as she sang along, lost to the music. I danced, too, moving my legs in opposition to my arms, the way Josie had taught me. We were a dancing family.

Occasionally Mom opened her eyes to watch me and hold her hand out to let me twirl. She threw her head back, laughing, then went back into the reverie that the music washed over her. *"Sha la la la la la la la la la la la tee dah,"* she sang. She swayed and moved around the room like a fine dress caught in a breeze. I thought she was the most beautiful thing I'd ever seen, dancing there in the shadows of the living room. I thought that this was maybe the happiest I had ever been in my whole life.

FOUR

While my mother and I danced, the shape of our family was changing without our knowledge. Although we could not have not known as much while we spun and laughed, two things were happening on opposite ends of the county that would mark us forever.

Now that I am grown, I can float like a spirit over the distance that separated us from my sister, who was at that moment watching a preview showing of *The Omen* at the Sky-Vu Drive-In on the other side of town. Knowing Josie as well as I do, I can imagine exactly what was happening with her that night, especially since she told me some of it later.

If I could have flown, I would have slipped out of our living-room window, floated down our road with the warm river by its side, and glided above the main highway, over Refuge's closed but well-lit businesses, the courthouse steeple's flag that rose and fell as if breathing in the thin summer breeze. Out into the darkness of the country again, over the high school and the spillway where teenagers went to park, over mountains becoming black with the deepening of night, and then to the drive-in, where the screen stood like an impossibly big and wide tombstone. The face of Gregory Peck loomed large there as he drew back the hair of his son's head and found the Mark of the Beast. Among the rows of cars — the movie was sold out that night — was a candy-apple red 1966 Mustang that belonged to Josie's boyfriend, Charles Asher.

Inside the car, Charles Asher was kissing Josie's neck, but she paid him no mind. She ate great handfuls of popcorn and kept her eyes on the movie. She paused from this only long enough to reach down into the floorboard for her Pepsi. She took a long drink, her lips capped around the straw for a moment after she was finished, and then set it back down without taking her eyes from the screen. Before leaving the house, she had shoved her flag pants into her big hemp purse and had changed into them as soon as Charles Asher picked her up. She had done so in the backseat, slapping Charles Asher's ear when he tried to watch her in his rear-view mirror as he drove away from our house.

Charles Asher—one of those people who is always called by his first and last names for no particular reason—was used to my sister not paying him very much attention. It was common knowledge that she had first gone out with him simply because he drove the sharpest car at the high school. After that initial date, she was taken by how he fawned over her, and then grew to like him, and then dislike him, but ultimately she felt such a mix of pity and gratitude to him that she was never able to quit him. He told me more than once that he thought he loved her, but he also knew that he'd never capture her heart completely.

Gregory Peck's demon-child, Damien, was running into a church and the horrifying music was rising, and Josie couldn't stand it anymore. She had snuck into a showing of *The Exorcist* when she was only twelve and had been forever scarred by that experience, so horror movies were not her strong suit, although she was scared of nothing else as far as I know.

Josie couldn't stand it anymore and had to look away. Only then was she completely aware of Charles Asher nibbling on her ear. She pushed him away, glad for this diversion. "Cut it out, Charles Asher," she said. "God almighty, you're like a dog in heat."

"I was just kissing you." Charles Asher straightened himself in his seat, his elbow knocking against the horn so that it let out a brief, halfhearted honk.

Josie ran the back of her hand down her neck. "You were slobbering all over me," she said, but then she realized how hateful she was being and felt a momentary pang of guilt. Later that summer she told me that it had taken her a long time to understand that the very reason she could never love Charles Asher was because he allowed her to treat him so badly. She could have never respected anyone like that. But that night she didn't understand why she sometimes detested him, no matter how much he bought her, no matter the long letters he wrote to her, confessing his undying love (she kept these in a cigar box under her bed, and I had read them all while she was out on dates). Really, she didn't understand much of anything at all.

Josie told me everything, even when I was very small, so I already knew that that summer she felt there might be something wrong with her. Any other girl at school would have killed for Charles Asher. He was good-looking in a JC Penney catalog sort of way, his face all angles and jutting bones, so that Josie sometimes had to look for the beauty there. His lips were his best feature — pink as the inside of a shell and plump as a girl's — but his brow was too high set and his eyes too far apart for her. The problem was, he wasn't interesting to look at, the way Steve McQueen or

Paul Newman were. She found beauty in irregularities, in roughness. Charles Asher had none that she could find; he was all perfection and smoothness. He was a good dresser, though, and drove this fine car and knew how to treat a girl, always buying her record albums and roses in little plastic sleeves. Josie preferred daisies.

She laid her head on his shoulder and tried to watch the movie again, but she had lost track of what was happening, although she could see that Gregory Peck was holding a knife up to stab someone.

"I didn't intend to be so mean," she said, and she felt his forgiveness wash over her so instantly that she had to fend off the urge to simply bolt from his arms and walk home from the drive-in. Why couldn't he ever fight back?

"It's all right," he said.

"Mom and me were into it again, before you came to get me."

"Over them stupid pants, I guess," he said. He had been through this before.

Josie sat bolt upright, mad again from thinking about it. "They're just pants," she said. "I don't see what the big deal is about the flag and all that."

"Because it's disrespectful for the flag to be worn. To be made into clothes."

"It's not made out of a real flag, for God's sake."

"Still, though," Charles Asher said, and looked straight

ahead at the screen, where the credits were beginning to roll. His father had been in Vietnam, too, so he often heard long lectures on the merits of patriotism and serving your country and good Americans versus bad.

"Still, what?" Josie said.

Charles Asher put his arm out across the back of the seat, Josie's hair as cool and soft as water against his fingertips. "It's just that we're different from other kids, because our fathers were over there. Nobody knows what something's like unless they've lived through it."

Josie looked at him for a long moment, seeing nothing. She hated his wisdom. Josie watched the credits roll and in that moment things changed for her. That is the exact moment when she began to question patriotism and Vietnam and everything that we weren't encouraged to question. That night, she told me, she realized that she was less like her father than the hippies he hated. She was thrilled by this discovery, but also filled with a sudden wash of panic.

Before this moment, she had always been Daddy's girl, his favorite in all respects. She had always sat on the arm of his chair while he watched the evening news, agreeing with anything Daddy said, whether it was his railing against something Ford had done or the legalization of abortion or his assumption that the whole moon landing had been faked. "They did it to get everybody's mind off the war," he always said, and nodded for emphasis. "Pretty smart."

Josie had always agreed with our father, and now she thought that she might not agree with him about anything anymore. It was a turning point in all our lives. Strange, how such a small realization can affect everyone's life forever. In movies there is always a carefully staged moment — a big crescendo of music, close-ups of the actors' faces, the camera slowly pulling away to let all this sink in for the viewer. Like the moment when Gregory Peck was about to kill the boy in *The Omen*. But in real life, most all of the extraordinary things happen with no more loudness than a whisper.

On the other side of the county from us, my father's turquoise Ford truck was making its way around the winding curves of the road from the train station in Black Banks. All was darkness in the cab of the truck except for a greenish rectangle of light that glowed from the radio and the circles of yellow light over the steering wheel, showing the speedometer. The radio was playing low, a country song that Daddy was vaguely aware of, somewhere in the back of his mind. He was more concerned with the woman sitting on the truck seat beside him, his little sister, and one of my favorite people who ever existed.

I can just see Nell. I bet she was smoking and leaning on the door, letting her face be pummeled by the good-smelling wind that rushed in her open window. Honeysuckles had bloomed all along the road that very morning, and the smell was so sweet that Nell wondered how such a fine thing continued to thrive in such a horrible world. She let this scent wash over her, hoping it would soak into her skin, even though she had really rolled the window down for the noise more than the fresh air. She didn't want to talk to Daddy and thought this might keep him from pushing her for answers. Like everyone else in our family, she was carrying a secret with her.

Daddy and Nell had once been very close, but I knew from many overheard conversations and one or two flat-out fights that they didn't get along because of the war.

While Daddy was in Vietnam, Nell had been a war protester. Eventually she had joined a march in New York City. She had carried a sign that read, GET THEM OUT NOW (I had seen a picture of this in a history book), and the fifty thousand people she walked with had sung "Blowin' in the Wind" and "We Shall Overcome" and chanted "Stop the Bloody War." The crowd had marched right up to the steps of the public library and lain down there, spread out so that the people trying to get in had to either turn away or step around them. They had lain there silently, hundreds of breathing corpses.

Eventually the police came with dogs and tear gas, and Nell was one of the many who were dragged away while CBS News and the Associated Press captured it all on film. She was seen all across the country, her body stretched between two police officers who were carrying her away by the ankles and wrists. She managed to wrestle one hand free so that she could thrust it toward the camera, two fingers fashioned into a peace sign. Her face was a scowl that became an image burned into the minds of everybody watching as Walter Cronkite narrated the scene. The photograph was on the front page of every newspaper in the country.

Nell's arrest had been the talk of the town, and several people wrote to Daddy while he was in Vietnam, informing him of his sister's actions. Some of them had even clipped the picture from the paper and enclosed it. Daddy never forgave Nell. Any argument between the two of them always led back to that day in New York.

"I did it for *you,*" Nell said one Labor Day when they were both drinking tall cans of Schlitz out on the back porch. They didn't even notice me, hovering near the kitchen door so I could eavesdrop on them.

"You did it to get on the news, for the thrill," Daddy replied. His best feature—his eyes—turned evil when he was mad, and he was giving her a murderous look. His speech was slurred. I had never seen him drunk before, and never would again. "Hippie."

"I didn't want my brother to come home in a body bag, Stanton."

"You're no better than those sons of bitches in Boston who spat on me when I walked down the street in my uniform."

Nell had put her hand on his arm and said, "But most of us weren't like that," in a motherly sort of voice, just as Daddy pushed her away.

"*Baby-killer,* they said." Daddy wasn't even aware of anyone around him by then, drunk on beer and memories. "*Baby-killer.* And spat on me."

Both of them were silently reliving that fight — although one of many, it had been the most honest — as they drove along the summer road, toward our house, where Nell would be living now. My father was not happy about this situation, but she was his sister, and despite how mad he still was at her, he couldn't let her go homeless. She wouldn't tell him what had happened, and he didn't press her for answers. She had called my mother and said she had quit her job and wanted to come home and needed somewhere to stay and that was all Mom had told him.

My mother was closer to Nell than Daddy, anyway. They had known each other since high school and were more like siblings than Nell and Daddy were. When Mom called Daddy at the gas station and told him about Nell, he knew the only thing he could do was drive over to Black Banks to fetch her. He had, and now they were on their way home, the song playing on the radio between them.

They didn't say a word as they pulled into our driveway, got out, and made their way around to the back door. Our music greeted them, flowing out the open windows.

FIVE

By the end of the song, my mother was fully spellbound. She held her arms over her head, shook her hair, let her head sway with the beat of the song. I was still dancing in front of her, but my heart wasn't really in it. I was more concerned with watching her, as if I was seeing her true spirit for the first time. Just as the song went off, we noticed that Daddy and Nell had slipped in, standing in the doorway between the living room and kitchen.

My father stood there with his hands on his hips. He was a big presence even though he wasn't a particularly big man. He had a natural charm that caused people to like him right away, as he seemed to always know the right thing to say. He thought out his sentences and then delivered them in a careful way that made people respect him, too. He was dark in every way except for his green eyes, which were green as walnut husks. If a person looked at them too long, they might be hypnotized. Daddy's whole face was smiling, and I knew it was because he liked to watch Mom dance. He looked only at her. But Nell winked at me.

"What're you all up to?" Daddy said in his laughing voice, the voice he had on good days, when the war wasn't right there behind his eyes. Although he was addressing both of us, he was really only speaking to my mother. He took a single step forward and gave her a kiss. Their lips lingered longer than necessary, long enough for her to bring her hand up and put her pointing finger into the cleft in his chin. This was her favorite part of his face, a fact she made well known. Daddy was still dressed in his work clothes, although the gas station he owned had been closed since five o'clock that afternoon. His hands were stained by work but she pulled them up to her face and kissed them although they were grimy with oil and gasoline. "I love it when you come home dirty," she said in a Mae West voice, and put her lips to each of his knuckles. Usually he washed up at work, but sometimes when he was in a hurry to get home, he came in like that. He kept a big plastic jar of hand cleanser that felt like lard and smelled like oranges on his shelf in the bathroom.

"Hey there, buddy," Daddy said to me.

I didn't answer at first, miffed that our dancing had been interrupted. But then I reconsidered, thankful that his voice was so easy tonight. "Hey," I said, but I could tell he didn't even hear me.

Mom folded Nell up in her arms. Nell shut her eyes and looked as if she were about to cry, both her hands lain so flat on my mother's back that I thought the cigarette stuck between Nell's fingers might ignite Mom's hair. Just when I thought Nell might shed a tear, Mom released her and held her by the shoulders. "Everything'll work out," Mom said, quiet. "I'll see to it."

Nell stepped around Mom and held both arms out for me. "You better come here, buddy." Her cigarette bobbed up and down in her lips when she spoke. "I need me some sugar."

"I'm too old to give sugar," I said.

Nell rushed across the room and lifted me onto the couch, her weight on me as she tickled my belly. "I'll have to steal it, then," she said, and twin lines of smoke escaped her nose as she laughed.

After tickling me for a while, Nell finally fell back against the couch, out of breath. She kept her arm stretched out across my shoulders. "I missed you. Haven't seen you in six months."

"Where you been?" I asked.

"Oh, Lord, baby," she said. "To hell and back, that's

where." Nell was quiet long enough for me to study her properly. She had long red hair and freckles all over her body, strewn out across her nose like a constellation. I liked that about her. She looked younger than she was, most likely because she acted so much younger than I thought a woman her age should act. Her lips never quite closed, so that you could always see her two front teeth, and I liked that about her, too. It made her look wild and carefree, which she was.

"Y'all must be starved," Mom said to Nell and Daddy. "I'll fry you some pork chops."

Daddy followed her into the kitchen, and this movement brought Nell back to earth, so she sat up and clucked me on the arm with her knuckles. "Hey, why don't you help me get my stuff out of the truck? I brought all my records, and you're allowed to listen to them anytime you want to."

She squatted down so I could latch my arms around her neck and be carried on her back. She stomped out of the living room and into the kitchen, where Daddy was sitting at the table, sipping a cup of coffee while Mom worked at the stove, warming up the macaroni and setting the cast-iron skillet on the stove. Daddy barely glanced our way as we went out the back door.

I buried my face in Nell's hair. She always smelled like the woods, like trees and rocks and wild things. Hers was a clean scent, spicy and green. I thought: I should remember this moment. I could write it down in my little composition book, the one that contained all my secrets that no one would ever read. I didn't know why, but I always felt the need to write about times like this evening when I had danced with my mother and rode Nell's back. Whole scenes of your life can slip away forever if you don't put them down in ink.

There were no streetlights out here in the country, ten miles from town, so the night was black and it took our eyes a moment to adjust. Nell caught sight of the starred sky as we stepped out into the yard, so both of us were looking up as she bounced me on her back out to the driveway.

"Country people sure do have more stars than anybody else," she said. "We ain't got much, but we got the stars."

The hills were full of the calling cicadas and katydids and crickets, but there was also the sound of an engine ticking in the driveway. Just as Nell reached the back of Daddy's pickup and let me drop onto the ground behind her, we both realized that Charles Asher's Mustang was parked in the driveway, too.

Then the sound of much fumbling about and the door popped open and Josie practically fell out, scrambling to run and hug Nell. Charles Asher fired up his engine and backed away. Josie was so caught up in her reunion with Nell that only I waved good-bye, his headlights sweeping over me.

"Oh, Nell, I'm so happy to see you," Josie said, then leaned down and kissed me on the forehead. She smelled like Hai Karate, the cologne she had bought when we went to the Rexall for Charles Asher's birthday. She had sprayed it on my wrist to test it.

"Don't you know better than to neck in your own driveway, though?" Nell asked. "What if your daddy had come out?"

"Shoot, he worships Charles Asher. He wouldn't care."

"He smells Charles Asher's cologne all over you, he'll care. Believe me, I know him well." Nell pulled a blue milk crate full of record albums out of the pickup and put them into Josie's hands. "He was my big brother and used to police every boy I went out with."

"He's still your big brother," Josie said, laughing, her face lit with the dim yellow light of the truck's interior light.

"All I'm saying is you better be careful." Nell left the door open and then climbed into the back of the truck, swinging her legs over the tailgate. "Here, Eli," she said, and handed me a small blue overnight case.

"You shouldn't have left the way you did tonight," I told Josie. "You hurt Mom's feelings."

"I don't *care*," she said, and even to me, she sounded like a spoiled brat.

"You should care," Nell said, hopping off the bumper, carrying a record player and several pairs of Levi's stacked atop it. As she went by the truck, she slammed the door shut with her foot. "Your mother has been through a lot for you."

"What's that supposed to mean?" Josie said, following Nell through the black yard.

"That means she'd do anything for you, and I know what I'm talking about," Nell said. "Be good to your mother."

We followed her back around to the screen porch through the black June night.

SIX

Everyone was talking about freedom that summer, but I knew what freedom truly was: riding my bicycle as fast as I could down the road, then letting go of the handlebars and gliding along with my arms outstretched. When done just right, this felt like flying. There is no freedom like one a child possesses, and that summer Edie and I were about as free as two people can be.

Every day was the same: we rode bikes up and down our road, back and forth, or carried rocks in the creek to

work on our dam, or sat within the shade of the big snowball bush where we drew pictures or played war with little
plastic soldiers or tried to read each other's minds. But
mostly we rode bicycles.

Sometimes the heat spread itself out over us without
our noticing. Before we knew it, the world was baking and
we were sweating so much from riding up and down the
road that we decided to go down into the shoals of the river
to cool off. That's the way it was the day after Nell arrived
at our house.

We parked our bikes and sat right down in the shallow
water that ran over round black rocks. I loved the way
denim felt when it got wet, so heavy and full of water. Once
you got blue-jean cutoffs wet, you could be cool for a long
while; it took them forever to dry. We pulled off our tennis
shoes so the water could wash between our toes.

After some splashing and then a long, thinking silence,
Edie looked up at me with concern. "I've been thinking,
about your daddy," she said. "What that must be like, to
hold all that in."

"Hold what in?"

"All that. About the war," she said, watching her toes as
she leaned back on her hands. Her arms were very straight
and long, already tanned a deep golden brown. "We studied
about Vietnam last year, in school. The worst things happened during that war, Eli. It's too awful to think about,
some of the things that happened."

"Like what?"

"Like little kids would come up to the men and have bombs strapped to them and they'd blow up. And monks burned themselves in the streets. And soldiers had to go into villages and kill everybody because they didn't know who was their enemy and who wasn't. And the men walked for ages and ages."

"Daddy's feet are all messed up because of that," I said, quiet. I had studied his feet many times. Some of his bones looked as if they'd poke right through the skin, and all his toes were mashed together, with his second toe popped up to rest atop his big one. They were awful to look at, so he rarely went barefoot, although the rest of us never wore shoes inside the house. Seeing his feet didn't disgust me, though. They made me feel like I was regretting something, but I didn't know what. You could see the war, right there in his feet.

"I heard him tell Mom that he once went for two whole weeks without pulling off his boots."

Edie leaned back on her elbows and brought one foot up out of the water, arching her leg so that it was high out in front of her. "I have really nice feet."

"There's no such thing as nice feet," I said.

She considered her foot, turning it this way and that, as if trying to catch the perfect light. "They're the only thing I'm vain about."

"What does that mean, *vain*?"

"Like stuck up," she said. "It's a good word. I found it in the dictionary." Edie was always finding words in the dictionary and trying to work them into everyday conversation. She slid her foot back into the water and looked at me. "Did he ever get shot?"

"No, but his back is full of shrapnel. My mother squeezes it out sometimes." Edie didn't know what it was, so I told her. "Little slivers of metal from the grenades. It looks like pencil lead."

Edie didn't reply, considering this. The sound of the water—like sizzling grease—churned between us, so we had to speak up to hear each other. "My aunt Nell came back home last night. She's going to live with us."

"They don't get along, though, do they?" Edie said. Last fall she was the one who had rushed onto the school bus, taken her seat beside me, and flipped open her history book to show me that Aunt Nell's picture was in there. Edie read the caption below the photograph: "This picture of a young protester became one of the most recognizable images of the anti-war movement and was instrumental in changing the nation's attitudes about the war in Vietnam." Edie had said that the most powerful thing was the way Nell wants people to look not at her but at the peace sign. If I looked at the picture long enough, I could imagine everything about that day. The way the street must have peeled away the skin of her face when they dragged her, the roar of the people, the police on their megaphones, the smell of the tear gas.

"Naw, they don't get along too good," I said. "But there's something wrong with her—I don't know what—and she's his sister, so he can't turn her away. That's what Mom told Stella."

Edie plucked a little rock from the riverbed and held it up to her face, looking for quartz. She turned it in the sunlight and brought it up to her mouth. Her tongue darted out and touched the skin of the stone. She had the habit of touching and tasting everything.

"My parents are getting a divorce," she said, just like that, then looked at me. I had heard of lots of people getting a divorce but had never known anyone who had. My parents didn't even like for me to watch *One Day at a Time* because the mother on there was divorced. I didn't know what to say, so I just looked at her. If I had been older, I might have told her how sorry I was or something. But in that moment I was helpless. There was no use in asking why, because everyone knew. If anyone needed to get a divorce, it was Edie's parents. They fought all the time. Loud. Sometimes on the front porch or in the yard. And even when they kept their fury contained to the house, we could all hear them screaming at each other.

Usually when this happened, Edie hid out in the high branches of her willow tree, or within our snowball-bush playhouse, or she came to our house and acted like nothing was happening. Once she had sat on the back porch with my mother and helped her with some microscope slides for Mom's class, carrying on an entire normal conversation about school while her parents raged through the walls of their house. Even though she had talked to Mom as if nothing was happening, when she got ready to leave, Mom wrapped Edie up in her arms and whispered, "If you ever need me, I'm here." I had never loved my mother more, but I had also felt a scratch of jealousy. It seemed she was never really there for me, not like that. It seemed she was aware of everyone's hurting except for mine. I was always thinking of when she had told Daddy she loved him more than anybody else in the world. I thought that should be me and Josie, not him.

"It's all right, though," Edie said, even while her face betrayed what she was saying. She looked down and sucked in on her lips, like she was trying to keep from crying. I had heard my mother tell Stella one time that it was easy to not break down unless you were talking to someone you loved. That's when you lost it.

I wish now that I had said something to make her feel better, but I couldn't think of anything. Instead, I said something more selfish than compassionate: "Does this mean you'll have to move off?" As soon as the words left my mouth, I had a rush of panic, thinking that she would definitely be leaving me, that she would have to go off to live with her mother somewhere else. I wanted to say, "I couldn't stand it if you left," but of course there was no way I was going to make that a known thing.

"No. I'm going to stay with Daddy," she said, and this was the only time her voice broke a bit. "My mother is leaving here, and she's not taking me with her."

"But you and him don't get along," I said.

"I don't get along with her any better, though. She's crazy, Eli. You don't know how lucky you are, to have a mother like yours. Everybody loves her. But my mother, she stays holed up in that house, thinking up things to be miserable about. Daddy can be a turd, but he's tried to be good to her. And it's impossible. She's impossible."

Edie stood up, streams of water falling from her shorts. "They don't realize I know yet," she said, and stomped across the riverbed. "They're planning on telling me tonight." She climbed up the fern- and ivy-covered bank with ease.

We rode our bicycles for a long time without speaking. We didn't talk or tell jokes or anything. Every once in a while Edie would zoom off in a burst of speed, her brown legs pumping with all her strength, her handlebar streamers crackling in the wind. We rode way out on our road to where the bridge spanned the part of the Refuge River that turned wild. My mother forbade us to set foot on this bridge, as it was too high and she knew that I had bad judgment when a danger presented itself. I was terrible about taking dares: if someone defied me to walk atop a bridge railing or jump off a twenty-foot-high cliff, I would. But we were already there, and I was desperate to see over the railings into the white water below. We stood behind the concrete railings lining the bridge and peered over. The water was more than thirty feet below us and didn't look like the Refuge River we knew. Hurried along by a couple of falls, the water sizzled over mossy rocks and fanned out in clear, wide arcs against bigger boulders that sat in its path. The sight of all that air between us and the river made my stomach jangle, and I knew I'd write about this later, in my composition book.

"That little boy haunts this place," Edie said. "Can you feel him?"

"No," I said, trying to convince myself. "Hush."

All of us children had heard the tale of the little boy who had plummeted to his death from this bridge, ages ago, in the 1940s. He was out for a walk with his mother and she was thinking about her husband, who was off fighting Germans. She was daydreaming and picking wildflowers beside the road, so he went on ahead. He got to the bridge and climbed the railings, thinking that it must be just like the fence that stood at their backyard.

"See? A rail here, and here, and here," Edie said, telling the story for the hundredth time. "And when he got to the top railing he thought he could just jump over onto soft grass, like on that fence at home. His mother looked up from her flower picking about the time he reached the top rail. She started running to him. I bet she dropped them flowers all in one big clump."

I could see her, too. I had imagined her many times, her hair falling down out of its pins when she ran. Her hands, white-knuckled, holding on to the railing while she peered over and saw her little boy lying on the rocks down there, already dead. I always wondered what happened then, how she made her way down to him, how she got help to come to her. I thought she had most likely gone down there and carried him back up the steep bank herself. I thought about this for a time. I bet myself that she fell down in the road with him stretched out across her legs. I could see every bit of it, playing in my mind like a movie.

"I can definitely feel him," Edie said, her eyes scanning the space around us in search of his ghost showing itself. "He stays here, I think."

"Shut up, man." My words came out like three quiet breaths.

Edie had frightened herself, too, and somehow we both knew to start pedaling at the same time. We pumped our legs hard to get as far away from the bridge as we could. I kept seeing the little boy, though, pausing atop the railings for one second before he stepped into air. I thought that he probably didn't have enough time to call out. I tried to stop myself from thinking about it or I'd end up obsessing about it all night long, the way I sometimes lay awake thinking about the end of time or eternity, which — even if spent in heaven — was bound to get boring at some point.

The June wind washed over us as we pedaled up and down our road, sometimes racing, sometimes riding with no hands. After a thick time of silence, I turned my transistor radio back on and we sung along with Melanie on "Brand-New Key," and before long Edie was laughing again.

SEVEN

The noon sun was burning at the top of the sky before I went home. I rode my bicycle into the backyard and saw my mother, but she was too far away to notice me. The garden was at the farthest corner of our backyard, and she was crouched in the dirt, studying her strawberry plants. Being a biology teacher, she approached everything like a scientist. She only raised fruits, which was unusual, as most people on our road worked big vegetable gardens full of dark-leafed tomatoes, leaf lettuce that was so bright and green it was almost yellow, and shady little pepper plants that shivered in the faintest breeze.

I watched her as I put down my kickstand. Mom stood and brought up a hoe that had been lying next to her, then immediately began to chop out any weeds that had popped up in the last couple of days. I liked to work in the garden, but not in the hot part of the day, so I went on inside to make myself a peanut-butter-and-jelly sandwich, a meal I would have lived on if I had been allowed to do as I pleased.

As I came around to the screen porch, I saw that Nell was still sitting there in her nightgown, drinking sweet tea, smoking a Winston, and reading a thick paperback with a bright orange cover. Her legs were folded out on the seat beside her, one elbow propped on the arm of the glider. She was far away, transported by the book, and she hadn't noticed my approach. Her face was as peaceful as a pasture, smooth and free of worry as she read. She took long draws from her cigarette, concentrating particularly hard until she blew the smoke back out.

I wondered what mystery lay behind her coming to us. We hadn't seen her in six months and now she was all-the-sudden here. She had stayed with us for short stints before, but this time she had brought all her albums and her record player and the few clothes she owned, so I knew she planned on staying awhile. Nell was always wandering around the country, never staying in one place long. She had lived in

Nashville and New York City, Atlanta and Boston. Sometimes my mother called her "a free spirit," in the kind of voice that let me know she approved of this lifestyle. For Nell, at least.

I opened the creaking door to the screen porch and stood there a solid minute while Nell finished the page. At last she laid the book facedown across her thigh. "Hey there, wild man," she said, as if I had just slipped in the door, and blew smoke out of her nose. "Where've you been?"

"Out riding with Edie," I said, and plopped into my mother's rocker. A breeze came down the valley and knocked the chimes together. "Why are you still in your nightclothes?"

She glanced down at her gown as if surprised she was still wearing it. "I didn't feel like getting dressed, that's why," she said. "I just wanted to smoke and drink sweet tea and read my book. That's just about the perfect way to spend a day, if you ask me."

"What is it?" I said, nodding my chin toward the book.

"A James Michener," she said.

"It's so big. I'd never in this world read all that."

"It has one of my favorite lines of all time in it: 'Only the rocks live forever.'"

"What's that mean?" I said. There was a scab on my ankle, so I reached down to pick at it while we talked.

"Well, I can only say what I think it means," she said. "To me it means that we might as well not worry about anything because we're all going to die, anyway."

"That's sad," I said, and at once wished that I hadn't replied in such a way. It seemed much too revealing. The scab picking was producing a pleasurable hurt. I lifted it too far, and a dark bubble of blood stood around the edges.

"It's beautiful, though, don't you think? Just the way the words go together? It's all perfectly chosen. 'Only the rocks live forever.' A good truth."

I appreciated that Nell was talking to me like a grown-up, but I had no idea what she meant. Still, I could see that the words flowed together like water over a riverbed. It was a phrase I would repeat in my head later on in the summer without really knowing why.

I took off my tennis shoes and brought my feet up under me, sitting Indian-style in the rocker. This produced a helpless feeling in my gut, rocking back and forth without my feet touching the ground. Somehow I knew that this was how Nell felt all the time, this wild stirring in the gut brought on by her own doings.

Nell stretched and let out a long yawn, her arms going out wide, her hands balled into fists. "I usually don't sleep so late," she said, midyawn. "But Josie and me set up all night, talking."

I had heard them laughing and whispering to each other, as their bedroom was right next to mine. For a while I had stood in my bed and pressed my ear to the wall, hoping to hear some secrets, but had caught only snippets and giggling.

"How long are you staying with us?" I asked.

"Why? Are you already sick of me?" She smiled and took a drink of her sweet tea, which she drank from my favorite glass, decorated with a picture of Casper the Friendly Ghost dressed as Paul Revere.

"No, I don't want you to ever leave."

She laughed at that and laid her head against the back of the chair. She closed her eyes and stretched, arms jutting out with hands curled into fists. "That may very well be the case," she said, "I might just stay here forever, if your daddy doesn't run me off."

"There's a picture of you in Edie's history book."

She opened her eyes, but didn't straighten up right away. She looked at me as if I had just announced that a nuclear bomb had fallen on Refuge. She didn't say anything, but the smile faded from her face.

"The one of you in New York City —"

"I know which one," she said, each word quick and measured, looking up at the porch ceiling. "Don't mention that to Stanton, all right?"

"I won't," I said. "I've known awhile, but I wouldn't tell him. It upsets him."

She took a deep breath.

I stopped rocking and felt a momentary defense for my father rise up in me. I was filled with the anger that he sometimes carried around behind his eyes, and I didn't know where it had come from. That's what it was like to be the child of a Vietnam vet, though: we're always caught between defending our fathers and not understanding them. "Do you feel bad, for doing that? For that picture?"

She sat up stiff again and a tenderness spread itself out over her face, centering in her eyes and moving outward until it had changed the whole shape of her forehead and mouth. "No, Eli, I don't. Not for a minute." She shook her head a little, as if she didn't even know she was doing it. She looked so pretty to me, the way her face had come down to a little patch of sunlight that was falling through the screen. A block of light spread across her freckled nose and turned her eyelashes golden. "You should never feel bad for doing what you believe in. Your daddy was off fighting in Vietnam, and he believed in that. And I was up in New York City, fighting against the war. And I believed in that."

I didn't know what to say, so I just looked at her, feeling stupid and too young and full of some kind of longing I could not put a name to.

"I hate that it hurt him," she said, quiet. "But at the same time, I wish he could see that I was doing it for him."

Then she sat back again, and her eyes drifted out over the yard to fall onto my mother. After a time I turned my head so I could see Mom, too. She had squatted down again, on her knees in the dirt, studying the strawberry plants. She had her hair pulled up in a tight bun, which made her look much older than she usually did.

"She's the best friend I ever had," Nell said, and I turned

back to face her. She had lit another cigarette and was still looking at Mom. "She's having a hard time out of Josie right now, you know."

I clenched my hands before me and stared at the way my fingers fit together. "I know it. They fight all the time."

"I tried to talk to Josie about it last night," Nell said, each word coming out with a blue puff of smoke. "But she's impossible sometimes. She just won't listen when she doesn't want to."

"I know all about that," I said.

"Lord have mercy, she's stubborn. Like Stanton."

"He says you're stubborn."

"Does he, now?" She laughed and took another draw off the cigarette. "He can't see that the real problem between us is that we're just alike," she said, but then shot me a surprised look, like she didn't mean to say such aloud.

"Where's Josie at now?"

"Lord, I don't know," she said. "Gone off somewhere with Charles Asher."

"He's rich."

"Is he?" She leaned forward a bit, as if genuinely surprised. "He doesn't act it."

"His daddy owns the hardware store *and* the drive-in. He was in the war, too. Somebody at school told Charles Asher that everybody who went to Vietnam got laid over there and took dope all the time."

"Well, that's not true." She looked at the cover of her

book and ran her hand over it, like someone wiping fog from a bathroom mirror.

"I know it," I said, my words darting out. I loved this story and wanted to tell the rest of it. I worshipped Charles Asher. "He busted that boy's mouth and got suspended for two days."

"Well," she said, "I guess he did what he believed in, too." And then she looked out on the backyard again, but it seemed to me that she was looking past my mother and the garden, past the ridge of good beech and hickory trees that rose up behind our house, even past the air, so thick with heat that it seemed like something solid one could walk through. I wondered what she was studying on, but figured it was something that grown-ups daydream about without realizing why.

To break this spell that had befallen her, I felt like I had to keep talking, so I asked her something I'd been wondering for a while now. "How come you never married?"

Nell didn't answer me, and I couldn't figure why. This seemed like a perfectly good question to me. Everybody else I knew her age was married, after all. She was still looking beyond everything, still caught up in some faraway thought that had carried her far away from me and the porch.

I repeated myself, louder this time. When that didn't work, I said "Nell" in a tone my teachers used when someone's attention had turned to the windows. And it worked, so she looked at me, startled. "What was it?" she asked. I asked my question for the third time.

She laughed and two little snorts of smoke came out of her nose. "Because I never wanted to get a divorce, I guess."

I didn't understand what this meant, but nodded anyway. I thought this was the adult thing to do.

"Not everybody has to get married, you know. I mean, it's not *required* or anything," she said, in that way she had of speaking when she felt very strongly about something. She felt strongly about many things. Somehow she seemed a bit miffed, too, but as soon as I thought this, a little smile showed on her face.

"Unless you want to have kids," I said.

Nell seemed at a loss for a reply, which was unusual for her, so she picked her book up off her thigh and held it in one hand before her face. "Well, you ought to get you something to eat. Go on, now, buddy," she said. "I need to read my book."

I left her there and went into the shadows of the kitchen. Mom had pulled all the shades in the house to keep the heat out as much as possible. We only had a small air conditioner that hung in the living-room window, but it was never turned on unless the heat became unbearable. Even then, it didn't do much more than cool the living room. Sometimes we would all stand in front of the sputtering white box, pulling our collars down so the cool air would wash over us. It hadn't been hot enough for that yet this summer.

I loved the kitchen when it was quiet and free of everyone else. It seemed to be the cleanest room in the house, with its scent of lemon Joy and the white stove, which was so shiny and clean it looked like something that ought to be in a doctor's office.

I took a loaf of Bunny bread from the breadbox and fixed myself another sandwich on a melamine plate. I shook out a line of Pringles in the space between the two triangles of bread. Nell had left the gallon jug of sweet tea out on the counter — she often forgot to put things away — so I poured some of that in a jelly jar.

I sat in the kitchen without turning on a light and ate, enjoying the quiet. Our house was not quiet very often, especially in the summer, when Charles Asher practically lived there and Stella would come in the door without knocking, already talking before she had pulled the latch, or Edie ran in to ask me to go somewhere. There was nothing now except for the *nit-nit-nit* of the stove clock and a redundant but comforting drip from the kitchen faucet.

Since it was so quiet, I could think properly, and I tried to chalk up things that I might do over the rest of the summer. I thought about how Edie had said I ought to ask my father about the war, but it seemed the better thing to do would be to venture into my parents' room and find the letters that Daddy had written to my mother while he was overseas.

I knew this would be wrong of me; my mother was very strict about no one ever going into their bedroom. But Daddy wouldn't ever say anything about the war, and now he was having these bad nightmares about it, and I needed to know more. I chewed on my sandwich and considered all the options and thought I would wait until the day after tomorrow, as I knew that Fridays — Town Day — were when my mother and Stella always loaded up and went to the Piggly Wiggly together. Daddy would be at work, and Nell and Josie were sure to be out doing something or other. I'd invite Edie to join me.

From outside I could hear Nell singing. I crept to the door and looked out. She had spread the book over her thigh again and was lying back now, her hands folded atop her chest like someone in a casket. Her eyes were closed, but she was singing, *"Go lightly from the ledge, babe, go lightly on the ground"*—the Bob Dylan song she played sometimes on her little green record player. Her folded hands patted out the beat on her chest. Listening to her, I realized that Nell was maybe the saddest person I had ever known, although she hid it. I thought maybe she was sad for the same reasons as me. Because sometimes, there was too much goodness in the world to bear.

EIGHT

Later in my life I would come to understand that history books are the least reliable witnesses. When I was ten years old, though, I believed everything that was taught to me at school. America was a completely generous presence in all regards. The Indians were heathen murderers who had to be driven out so we could settle the nation in a civilized, God-blessed fashion. The Revolution was a war fought in smart blue and red uniforms wherein men with freshly powdered wigs acted as gentleman while they killed one another. The Civil War was as simple as the North fighting the South to free the slaves. America had saved all of humanity in both world wars, with little help from anyone else.

Although I bought everything that the history books doled out to me, I never completely believed my own parents' love story. Whenever they talked of those first months when love bloomed up between them, there were always a few things they didn't talk about. The whole story of their romance—as told by them—was a jigsaw puzzle with pieces that had been badly cut out and could never make a solid square.

But I was an expert at eavesdropping, so I knew the real story, although none of them realized how much knowledge I possessed. This is the true story, with some of what they told us thrown together with the things I overheard while hiding beneath the porch or pausing at doorways or hovering at corners.

My mother, who had no family at all, had been raised at the Refuge Methodist Children's Home, which was a fancy name for an orphanage. All she knew about her family was that her mother had come there, pregnant and unwed, at sixteen and had fled the day after the birth, never to be heard from again. So she was a girl completely alone in the world. Because she excelled in the orphanage school, she was handpicked by the home's director—a stark-looking but tenderhearted woman called Miss Feltner—to receive a scholarship that enrolled her in the private high school run by Kate Sloan College. There were only twenty-five people in her graduating class, and my mother hadn't liked a one of them. "They were all snobs," she'd say. "They all thought they were better than me because I was an orphan."

While Miss Feltner and her staff had always been good to her, my mother had never known what it felt like to have a family until she wandered into the House of Wax, the record store on Main Street, and found Nell working there when they were both seventeen years old. Although my mother was a little bashful and Nell had never met a stranger in her life, something clicked between them and they became instant friends.

(What was always left out of this story as told to me was that my mother was two months' pregnant at the time. I was hidden beneath the supper table when my mother told all of this to Stella, with Stella's knees an inch from my face. I don't know why she didn't feel me breathing on her legs.) "I just went wild that year," Mom said. "I guess I felt like nobody loved me, and I wanted some attention, and I ended up pregnant by this boy who didn't care anything for me, and I didn't him either." He left the day after their high-school graduation, never to be seen again.

Hearing this story filled me with a dull kind of grief. This was heavy knowledge for a little boy to carry, but we all have some kind of load like this as children, and we all bear it the best we can. All I could think of was Josie, and whether she knew.

Nell took Mom home with her, and that's when Mom first saw Daddy. My mother liked to say, very often, that she had never felt as free in her entire life as she did that day. Sitting in Nell's mother's big red Buick, one arm propped in the open window as she watched the town slip away and the countryside open up on either side of them, like a green, busy hymnal spread out, its spine the road. High summer. "There were tiger lilies all down the side of the road," she'd remember, and I imagined great orange-red waves that bobbed and swayed in the wind of the passing car. Nell's house was out on the river and my mother had never been allowed out there before. Everyone she knew believed that if people didn't live in town, they weren't worth knowing. She did not agree.

They raced down the winding road, bouncing across the rickety bridge, plowing through the rising dust of the dirt road that led to Nell's house. She sped around this curve and that one until she came to a jaunting stop near a small white house.

"This is it," Nell said and when the dust fell away, settling on the big leaves of the big trees all around the yard like sifted flour, my mother stepped out of the car.

And that's when she first saw my father. He was bent into the engine of his truck, with no shirt and grease smeared up his arms. He wiped his hands on his pants and shook her hand, smiling. "I knew, right then," Mom said when she looked back on that day.

Meeting Nell and Daddy's own mother, Yvonne, was almost as good. Yvonne was a tall, long-fingered woman who was always in motion. Her husband had been killed in World War II, and she had found no need for another man in her life. "I got by just fine without him," she liked to say. She died before I was old enough to remember her, but was always a legend in our family.

After supper, my mother insisted on helping with the dishes. Afterward, they all sat on the porch drinking sweet tea, and Nell and Yvonne sang hymns to the gathering dusk. Yvonne kept an orange-and-black Gibson guitar propped up on the porch glider, which she snatched up before every song to strum out the key they would sing in, a capella. They closed their eyes as if no one else was there and harmonized what Yvonne called "gloaming songs," which is where my mother first heard her favorite word. They sang:

"Now the day is over, night is drawing nigh;
Shadows of the evening steal across the sky.
Now the darkness gathers, stars begin to peep;
Birds and beasts and flowers soon will be asleep."

While they sang, my mother thought she might have stumbled upon some enchanted place where people sang when they wanted to, and laughed while they were together, and actually enjoyed one another. She had never witnessed such a thing in her whole life. "And Lord, their voices," Mom said every time she recalled that evening. "It was almost too much to bear, it was all so good." By the time they started singing "Softly and Tenderly" to the graying world, she couldn't help it: she started singing with them. For the first time in her life, she didn't care if she was a good enough singer or not. She just wanted to sing, and when she did, Yvonne and Nell both smiled and nodded to her, egging her on until she sang with complete abandon.

When the song was over, Yvonne told my mother she was welcome to their home anytime. "We've eaten together, and we've sung together," she said, "so we're family now."

Then Yvonne grabbed the Gibson and sang "You Are My Flower" with her eyes closed, her left hand sliding up and down the fingerboard like an expert guitarist.

Later that night, my mother thought of what Yvonne had said about them being family. She lay in the twin bed across from Nell's, unable to sleep because of her joy.

After only a few visits, she found herself sitting on the back porch with my father, alone. "We talked about *everything*," she'd say.

He was already crazy over her by the time she told him that she was three months' pregnant. So there was no turning back. "He said it didn't matter," Mom told Stella. "He said the past was the past and that everything would be fine. He even said he'd treat the baby just like his own. He promised."

Stella leaned forward, causing her knees to loom danger-
ously close to my face. "And did he?" she asked. Apparently my mother nodded. "Well, that's all anyone can
ask," Stella offered. (Was it possible that something so large
was handled so simply? With my father it was. When he
loved someone, that was all that mattered. Mom had turned
eighteen and was able to leave the orphanage, so it was all
decided. Besides, he had some news of his own: he had
already enlisted.)

My parents were married in my grandmother's living
room. I have studied the picture of that day many, many
times. They're both looking right into the camera, leaning
into each other. Already they are a part of each other, as if
shoots of light are evident there between them, connecting
them. My mother is wearing a straight blue dress (there is
no sign of so much as a bump, much less a pregnant belly)
with a white rose corsage pinned high above her heart. She
has a stiff white collar and high heels, and her face looks
exactly the way it did when she was dancing. My father is a
movie star in a plaid blazer and tan slacks. He looks like
Paul Newman and has pennies in his loafers. What I love
most is the way they are holding hands, like people in an old
painting: his palm out as if cupping a cool drink of water,
my mother's hand lying atop it, straight, yet relaxed.

Daddy went off to basic training and came back home
for a week, and then, somehow, my mother found herself in

Fort Hood, Texas. She was excited that this was where Elvis had done his training when he served in the army only six years before. She took up housekeeping, all the while knowing that she would someday be able to take the college classes that would make her into a science teacher. This is all she had ever wanted to be her whole life.

Six months later, Josie was born in Texas. On that day my father was the first one to hold her. Mom told Stella that when the nurse laid her in his arms, she saw a jolt run all through him. "She's *ours*," Daddy whispered, not taking his eyes off Josie.

Those four years were a time of change for everyone. Nell kept on working at the House of Wax and was working there the day Kennedy was shot. She closed the store and rushed home to Yvonne, who was devastated, inconsolable.

On one of those long summer evenings when I was ten, Nell told me that on her way to work in March of 1965, she heard something on the radio news that changed her life. She heard the report that an eighty-two-year-old Quaker woman named Alice Herz had set herself afire on a Detroit street corner in protest of the impending war in Vietnam. Once Nell got to the record shop, she clicked off the radio, then the engine, and sat there a long while, listening to the cooling click of the motor and picturing this old woman dying in such a way. And she knew what she would have to do.

Right around that same time, Daddy came home one day with an important announcement. My mother was washing dishes while Josie played at her feet. Her hands became still in the warm dishwater. "No," she said, a single word she thought would do the trick, but he didn't budge. Then: "They won't make married men go overseas."

"I volunteered," Daddy said, and put his hand on her damp wrist.

She jerked away from him and took a step back, holding on to one of the wheat-patterned plates that Yvonne had bought for their wedding. She turned the plate in her hands as if sliding her fingers over a steering wheel. "Why would you want to do that, Stanton? It don't make no sense."

He told her that it felt like the right thing to do. He believed in fighting for his country. He had always longed for an adventure, and now one loomed before him. Plus they needed the money. A particular kind of patriotism, promises of adventure, finances. This is how boys end up soldiers.

"But it's getting bad," Mom said. "Real bad. Men are getting killed every day. It's all over the news." Her voice grew jagged and loud and she kept backing away from him, holding on to the plate. "Have you lost your mind?"

"They'll end up sending me anyway, Loretta," he said, his hands still out in front of him. "Come on now, baby. This way I'll only be over there a year. If I wait for them to send me, I'll have to go for two years."

"No!" she screamed, and slammed the plate onto the floor for emphasis. The plate broke into six neat pieces, one of them scattering across the floor to rest very near Josie's bare foot. Josie started crying and my mother gulped, "Oh, my God," realizing what she had done. She bent and gathered up Josie and stormed away.

(The thing that neither of them realized was that she was carrying me, too. She had become pregnant only the week before.)

When Mom remembered that day, she always recalled that President Johnson was on the television later that evening. She was so struck by part of what he said that she wrote it down and put it under a piece of sticky cellophane in her photo album. President Johnson said: "I do not find it easy to send the flower of our youth . . . into battle. . . . I have seen them in a thousand streets of a hundred towns in every state in this union—working and laughing and building, and filled with hope and life. I think I know, too, how their mothers weep and how their families sorrow."

After Daddy left for Fort Devens, Massachusetts, where he received special training before being flown to San Francisco (where he would board a boat that would carry him across the Pacific), my mother drove their green Corvair—loaded with Josie and everything they owned—for twenty hours straight. She staggered into Yvonne's house at three in the morning and collapsed on the kitchen floor.

Three months later she was certain that I was growing in her belly. About this same time, the first major antiwar rallies were being held in forty American cities. My mother and Nell and Yvonne watched the news coverage of the battles and the marches while the evening mists seeped in over the river. Often they prayed together, too.

Yvonne and Mom became very good at praying, but Nell's requests to God were often interrupted by the nagging fire of revolution that had been recently lit in her stomach. She couldn't stand just sitting there watching Walter Cronkite while the world went up in flames. She had to do something.

Nell had another clear memory of listening to the radio in November 1965, when she heard that four hundred soldiers had been killed in one ambush, at Ia Drang. "I drove straight on over to the college," I heard Nell tell Josie once, "and found the student group that was organizing protests." Ten days later, thirty-five thousand people marched against the war in Washington. Nell was one among them.

I had never heard Nell talk about her times on the road, roaming around the country fighting for peace or falling in love or the many other things she did. And my father never ever talked about the war. No amount of eavesdropping ever gave me that. All I knew about those two things were that Nell floated around and came back home occasionally and that Daddy served his time, got out of the army as soon as his tour of duty was over, and came back home for good.

So, in many ways, the most important parts of the stories were blank pages for me. And although I was good at making up my own tales to fill in the holes, I was never really able to do that with either Nell or my father. I knew that my imagination was not nearly good enough to envision what either of them had gone through, even when I tried many years later. Ultimately reality is far worse and far better than anything that either adult or child can ever dream.

NINE

After much thought, Nell had decided she needed a toothbrush, but it was important that she go to the Rexall and pick it out herself. Josie wanted a new bathing suit, and although she said it would be much cooler if Charles Asher would come and take her to town, my mother insisted that she had to help her choose the suit, since Josie would come home with a bikini otherwise. After the big gas shortages of a couple years before, smart people like my mother only went into town once a week, so after enough planning to take a trip overseas, she and Stella and Nell and Josie all loaded into my mother's amber-colored Cougar and drove into Refuge for groceries, swimwear, and a toothbrush.

I was lectured to stay close to the house. Even though I was no baby, Mom had never completely gotten over seeing *The Lindbergh Kidnapping Case* on television a few months ago and stayed in fear of my being snatched away. I acted as if I was put out by her concern, but secretly I relished these moments of motherly action on her behalf.

I stood in the front yard and waved to them as if they'd be gone a very long time, and as soon as they were out of sight, I sprinted to Edie's and found her sitting by her willow tree.

Edie wasn't crazy about the idea of going into my parents' bedroom, but her curiosity outweighed her trepidation, so she followed along when I told her what I wanted to do.

When we made our way into my parents' bedroom, my stomach flipped up at the corners. I knew what an invasion of privacy I was committing. I didn't fear being caught; instead I dreaded lying awake and feeling guilty about this for nights to come. We were not a family who went to church much — both my parents believed that God could be best served by being the best people they could and treating everyone right and being thankful for all they had — so my guilt was not the kind that is created or fostered. I was simply made that way: a boy who cared too deeply for everything and therefore felt that any wrong in the world was partly my fault. In retrospect I see that this is a good way to be, but it also makes for a miserable existence.

The shades were drawn so that their room was as dark and cool as a cave. Everything was immaculate. My mother couldn't stand to go anywhere without first making her bed. On the dresser, one side was devoted to Daddy's cologne and a leaf-shaped dish that held tie tacks (which were never worn, since he never wore ties). The other was reserved for Mom's Charlie perfume, a bowl for hair barrettes, and last year's picture of Josie and me, which had been taken at the fire department. In the middle sat the big cedar box that my mother had bought in Texas. I had seen her carry important things into her bedroom, bound for the box, enough to know that this was her hiding place for letters and souvenirs.

I put my hands on either side of the box and sat in the floor, Edie nearby. When I lifted the lid, the scent of cedar washed up over our faces, musky and cold, like the inside of an ancient tree.

In the box were my parents' marriage certificate, both my and Josie's birth certificates, a collection of movie-ticket stubs, a dried-up flower that looked like a shrunken, darkened version of the rose my mother had worn on her wedding dress. There was a ring with a small, brownish pearl; three of my or Josie's baby teeth in a baby-food jar; and a yellow Juicy Fruit wrapper that had *I am yours* written on its white side in slanting, cramped pencil. This was my father's handwriting, which I liked to study on the little receipts he wrote out for his customers at the gas station garage. There were deeds and insurance papers and many saved Hallmark cards (mostly from my father) and a postcard from the Mississippi University for Women with *I am here if you need me* scrawled across the back. And below all of this was the stack of letters, bound together by a black ribbon. The letters were housed in small white envelopes that had red-and-blue borders around the edges. Each was addressed to my mother, and in the upper left corner was a San Francisco Army Post Office Box number. In the space where the stamp should have been, my father had written *Free.* The packet felt as heavy as a big rock in my hands.

"We shouldn't be doing this," Edie said. She had slid down to the floor and sat leaning against the bed, her arms wrapped around her knees. "It feels wrong to me."

"Don't you want to know what it was like, though?"

She looked troubled, her normally blue eyes turned into dots of thundercloud gray. Her face was flat and square. "Yes, but not like this. You ought to just talk to him, Eli."

"He won't tell me anything."

"Maybe if you asked him the right way."

"I've asked every way I know how."

She sighed, her shoulders coming down with the long breath. "Well, maybe just a couple, all right?"

I worked the first letter out of the stack, afraid that if I undid the knot on the black ribbon my mother would somehow detect my intrusion. It seemed that she had arranged them from the earliest to the latest date after he had finally shipped out, since the first one was postmarked October 28, 1966. I brought the crisp envelope up to my nose and drew in its scent. The paper smelled of ink, tangy and metallic.

My mother had ripped the end off each envelope. I could see her doing this, careful and hesitant so as not to accidentally cut into the letter that stood inside. I tapped the corner against my palm, and the letter slid out. For just a moment I let the three pieces of small, folded stationery rest on my palm, testing their weight.

"Be careful," Edie whispered, making me feel as if I were handling a pack of firecrackers.

I unfolded the pages in slow, measured motions, and then laid them on the floor in front of me, smoothing my hand over the creases. The paper was thin and rough, like the paper I imagined the Constitution might have been written upon. I leaned forward on my knees and read aloud.

Hey Baby,

Well, I'm here. Six days on that ship. The first two days I was so sick I thought I was going to die. All these men who had gone through rough-as-hell basic training leaned over the rail, puking their guts up.

But I'm here. And I'm alive. So far. We are close to the Michelin and Firestone plants, which is a strange thing to know, being so far away from home and seeing the signs of something so familiar. I am missing you like crazy and somehow seeing those rubber factories makes me miss you all the worse.

My sergeant says that homesickness is what kills you over here, and also what gets you through it. As I write this I have been here two days and already I know that the main reason I want to live is so I can get back to you, back to home. I miss that soft place behind your knee and the way your mouth always tastes like strawberries.

"Eli," Edie said at this point. "Maybe you ought to stop."

But I kept reading:

I miss Josie getting my hand just before bedtime and asking me to take her out onto our little porch to see the stars. How quiet she was when I pointed out the Big Dipper to her, the way she sat up real straight and said, "I see it, Daddy," after a long time of looking, and the way it felt when I thought that maybe she did see it. God, you've never known homesickness until you're on the other side of the world. Add to this that you know you'll eventually see some action, that people are dying over here every day. If a man thought too much about it he'd get himself killed, as he'd crack up.

"That's enough, Eli," Edie said. I saw then that she had unfolded herself during my reading and was lying on the floor, one arm propping up the side of her face. "Come on, now."

"No," I said, and I didn't sound like myself at all. I never spoke with so much force to Edie. "Just a couple more."

But then I read three more, aloud, and after that she didn't stop me. With each one we went deeper and deeper into Vietnam. There was one about how they had to go into the jungle for two weeks, another about the way the B-52s would zoom in over them and bomb the Viet Cong. After that my father had to go on what he called search-and-destroy missions, although he never explained exactly what that meant. It seemed to be an understanding between him and my mother that he wouldn't spell out every single thing. He mentioned being dropped from helicopters into bamboo grass that was eight feet tall.

He talked about stringing Constantino wire around the camp, about building a bunker out of rubber trees and sand-bags. In one letter a small newspaper article from *Stars and Stripes* fell out. The entire first sentence was underlined in fat blue ink: *A Viet Cong forward aid station was discovered while on a search-and-destroy mission 15 miles south of Phuoc Vinh by Company A, 1st Batallion, 2nd Infantry, 1st Infantry Division.* A shaky arrow snaked out to the margin where my father had written in matching blue ink: *Our brigade.*

One letter detailed the prisoner of war my father had to

guard. The POW was tied up with rope in the center of a big field, with a soldier on each corner. There were long declarations of homesickness and admissions of fright and descriptions of the land and the people. My father wrote that in Saigon there was an old Vietnamese man who spoke perfect English and cooked a wonderful meal of rice and shrimp for my father and his buddies. The old man's teeth were solid black from opium, and he ate three fish heads while they feasted on their supper. "He could squat down for hours on his haunches," Daddy wrote. He told of children who stood beside the roads as the troops passed, all dressed in long sleeves no matter how hot it was. My father and the other soldiers broke Hershey bars into five pieces and handed them out. He told of riding for miles up and down Highway 1 in the back of army trucks while the land sped by.

And always the trees; he was obsessed with them. Especially their leaves. Their bigness, slickness, the way some of the leaves would hold rain like cups and leaves that were slender as green beans and smelled musky and sweet at the same time. Each letter was different in some way except that he always talked about the trees and he always said how much he missed my mother and Josie. He longed to touch my mother's pregnant belly.

The thing that struck me the most about all these letters was his love for the trees.

I knew that he could name any tree he saw. He was apt

to be walking along somewhere and nod in the direction of a beech and speak its name, or run his hand down a scaly bark and say, "Hickory" or peer far up into the branches and say, "Look, a persimmon tree." But he did this same thing with cars, too. Often when I was at a station with him, he would stand outside beside the Pepsi machine and watch as people sped by on the highway and sometimes by only the sound of the approaching engine he'd say, "'66 Mustang," or "Ford LTD," or "1971 Plymouth Duster." So I never knew that he loved the trees as much as I did.

This undisclosed connection that bound us now, the secret trees that neither of us spoke of to each other; it seemed like something that would be easy for a son and father to talk about. I lingered on this a long while after the fourth letter, thinking it over while the room grew smaller and darker and Edie relaxed into the silence of the house so much that she all but disappeared to me.

"One more, then," she said, at long last. Still quiet, still a whisper. I loved her for her quiet, for her lack of interference. I wanted to tell her how much I loved her for it, but I thought this would be a crazy thing to do and she would only punch my arm and laugh in that jaunty, menacing way of hers.

So I opened the one that would change me forever.

Dearest Loretta,

I usually start your letters with Hey Baby but I need to use your name now. I've been whispering it to myself all day long. Loretta Loretta. That's all that's gotten me through this day, saying your name, a name that I love because it's yours, because when I say it I see you in front of me.

I need to tell you something that I shouldn't. But I have to, because you're the only one who really knows me. Besides my mother and Nell, I know that you're the only person in this world who truly loves me. Some of these boys over here love me. I know that, too. We are like a family now. But if they live and go back to their families they'll probably only remember me every once in a while, for some strange reason they can't explain. I love them, too. They're the best friends I ever had because we're here, together, and you can't help but get close in times like these. But you know what I mean. When it comes right down to it all I have in this world is you and Josie and the baby and my mother and sister.

You can tell that I'm beating around the bush, so I'll just say it. I killed a man today. I have had to do some terrible things on those search-and-destroy missions, Loretta. Things I'll never get over. But today, I saw his eyes.

We were on a march up Highway 1. And I stepped aside just for a second to pee, although we're not supposed to do this, and just as I unzipped, there he was. Looking right at me and I could see in the way he

*clenched his jaw that he was about to pull his trigger
and so I pulled mine first and he fell not five feet from
me. Like his knees had been shot out from under him,
but the round hit him square in the chest and he was
dead just like that. He was about my age, probably a
couple years younger, but I bet he had a wife and family
and a mother and sister, too. We're not supposed to
think about that, but who can help it? I keep seeing his
eyes. They were so tired. And so then I say your name so
you'll come up and overtake his face.*

*So everything is changed for me, see. I won't go on
about it, but I had to put it on paper. A confession, I
guess. Don't ever speak of it again, all right? Let this be
the time I tell you and let it go.*

*This is a war, though. And until you're over here
you can't know what that's like. Nobody can. We keep
hearing on the news about the people marching against
the war and all that and even though some of them say
they're marching for us I just don't get it. I don't know
about all this either, all this war. But I do know that
I'm a soldier and I was asked to come here and fight for
reasons that my country said were right and so that's
my job now. That's what we're here to do and I'm here
now so I'm going to do it and just pray your name until
it's over. I don't have much light left, so I'll close,
although I could go on just writing and writing until it
was nothing more than nonsense. If I could do that*

maybe it would all start to make sense. But I don't
think so.

Burn this, Loretta. Loretta Loretta Loretta.

All my love,

Stanton

Less than halfway through the letter I had stopped reading aloud, but Edie was sitting close to me by then — we had both sat upright with our legs crossed, leaning over the letter on the floor in front of us — and she read a paragraph but then couldn't go on so we both read it silently, together. When we had read the last word, his name, we both sat there for a time without saying anything. The first thing I felt was sorry for him. I felt awful for him, to know that he carried that around with him every day of his life. That and more. Then I felt wrong and stupid. I didn't know what I was supposed to feel and why I felt the way I did. And then I was mad because he had never told me this, although I don't know what would possess a man to tell such a thing to his ten-year-old son.

Finally, Edie broke the silence.

"Oh, God, Eli," she said, and bolted away from me, realizing that we had gotten so close that our shoulders and the soles of our shoes were touching. "We shouldn't have done this. We shouldn't have read these letters."

I didn't say anything. I folded the letter and put it back in its envelope, then returned it to its proper place in the stack, planted it back in the sweet-smelling box, dropped all the other things atop it, and eased the box closed, as if lowering the lid on a living thing that is to be hidden away. I held the box with the flats of my palms on either side and sat it back down, caught a glimpse of myself and Edie in the dresser mirror, and left the room without a word.

I went to my beech tree on the ridge overlooking our house. Nobody knew I had this secret place of my own, not even Edie. I don't know why I didn't want to tell her that I had a tree, too, just like she had her willow. When she showed me that morning how to listen to the willow, I had already known. I had done the same thing many times with this tree.

I had read all about beech trees in one of the botany books my mother had kept from teacher's college. Their bark is not like bark at all, but skin. It doesn't ever get cracked and rough because the outside grows when the tree grows. So the trunks of beech trees sometimes feel alive, like an elephant's wide, gray legs. I appreciated beeches in particular because their leaves don't fall off in the autumn but cling to the branches until new, bright green leaves come back in the spring. All through the winter the brown, shriveled autumn leaves hang there, staying with the tree. The beech is never alone. This, too, made me feel as if the beeches were more alive than other trees, the way they long to have company, just like people.

When I had left our house, I had grabbed my composition book and walked in a determined, fast stride across the backyard, right through the garden. Edie had run down the steps of the screen porch, calling my name, but when I didn't turn to her, she had let the door slam behind her and sat down on the steps, watching as I walked away. I had known that she wouldn't follow me if I didn't invite her. And she had known that I needed time alone. From up there I could peer through the leaves and see our back porch, and I saw that she had finally tired of waiting for me to come back and had gone home. I hated to leave her like that, but I knew she'd understand. That was the best and most unexplainable thing about our friendship. Sometimes it was like we could read each other's minds. We never spoke about this, but both of us knew that we were constantly sending each other messages.

I knelt at the base of the tree and put both my hands against it. Its skin was cool, just as it always was, no matter how hot the weather. If I stayed very still, I could feel juices flowing within. I ran my hands down the trunk, the way the doctor had the time everyone thought I had broken my leg jumping off the toolshed roof. With my hands on the tree, I could feel what seemed like tendons, slight rises where the trunk felt as if it was flexing long, broad muscles.

After a while I leaned my head against the beech and let its coolness sink into my forehead. When I did this, I didn't have to think about anything at all. I just let the calm that the tree always possessed spread through me, and for a brief time I had no thoughts of my father killing a man, or of a war I didn't understand, or anything else. I thought only of the tree and the cool peace against my own skin.

After a time I turned and sat down, my back resting against the beech, my knees drawn up to my chest. I sat as still as I could and looked around me. Sitting down this way, I couldn't see any of the houses below me or anything except for a forest of leaves. Above me there was only bird-call. Redbirds that perched on a dogwood limb and peered down at me before fluttering away. A swallow that sang high in the branches of the beech. The forest was filled with birdsong and the cry of lone cicadas, mourning the oncoming heat of another June day. The world smelled different here. Clean and musky, like damp sand. I closed my eyes and saw my father bringing his gun up, saw the color drain from his face after the shot was fired. Heard the silence filling the jungle after the blast. I imagined colorful birds flapping away with much noise. I saw it all in my mind—every detail enlarged, exaggerated—so I opened my eyes and flipped through the pages of my composition book until I found the clean page where I had left my ink pen. I put the tip of the pen to the paper, but nothing came to me. There were no words.

I concentrated on everything around me.

Lifting a small sandstone rock near me, I found a colony of beetles, going about their daily routines. Scurrying away from the sunlight, disappearing into holes that looked far too small for their sudden escape. Some of them lazed about, though, content with some bit of food too tiny for me to see. And then I could run my hand over a clump of moss — so green it didn't seem real, as if all the green of the woods had soaked into it — and I knew that beneath my palm a whole world existed, a world made up of insects for which I knew no names. All these little live things. How many of them had I killed with my innocent footsteps to this place? I had most likely disrupted thousands of lives, obliterated things I wasn't even aware of. This pained me to think on.

Above me there were all the birds calling to one another. But beyond them there were hundreds of birds who sat silently, watching, waiting. And most likely dozens of snakes and lizards and other animals who were aware of me without my having any knowledge of them. I imagined that farther up the ridge, where the outcropping of gray rock stood like a row of clumped, crooked gravestones, a fox was watching me. I was so sure that I was being observed that I closed my eyes, picturing him. I thought he was a child-fox, and I could see each of his fine whiskers on either side of his nose, his brown eyes that had a spot of yellow in each one. His orange coat was clean and shiny. The white that smudged around his face lay like a soft shield on his chest. I imagined that he was considering me, wondering why I looked so sad.

The little fox may or may not have been there. I like to think that he was, and that after a long while he slinked away, wishing that we lived in the kind of world where he could comfort me.

Through the treetops I could see a whitening sky, a sky bleached by a boiling noonday sun. But here, within the leaves, the earth breathed up a thin chill. I could not cry for what had happened to my father, for what my father had done, so instead I curled up at the base of the tree, lay my head against one of the larger roots, and tried to not think about it. Sometimes just being still is the best thing you can do for yourself.

TEN

By late June the world was awfully hot, and everything suffered. The heat hung like a mist over the mountains. The leaves baked and drooped on the trees. The river shrank in places, revealing nakedness in the shoals, where only two thin streams of water trickled through. The swimming hole downstream remained full, but the water was still and stagnant-looking, moving only at the banks when someone jumped in from one of the cliffs.

Hardly anyone had an air conditioner, and those who did found it had very little effect on any part of the house except the room it was in. Whole families spent the hot part of the day gathered in whichever room this happened to be. Others threw open their windows and propped box fans in their open doorways to deal with the heat.

My family had no intention of being cooped up in the living room throughout most of the day — we were way too restless for that — so we simply accepted it.

Nell and Josie spent much of their time on lawn chairs in the shoals, parking themselves in the middle of the water and occasionally putting their hands down to cup water over themselves. Nell was very white and freckled. She wore a black bathing suit with a little skirt around the waist, but Josie, who was dark as a Cherokee, had on her two-piece that Daddy had about died over her buying at the Fashion Bug, even though Mom had relented and approved. The suit was pink with ties on each hip, which gave the illusion that one tug of the strings could make the bottoms fall away.

Nell and Josie wore matching white sunglasses (Nell had bought them at the Rexall) and slathered themselves in baby oil they had spiked with iodine. Everybody did it that way then. They lay back with their arms very straight at their sides. Josie had brought along a small radio that she tied to the back of her lounger with a shoelace. The music was distorted by the time it reached the hiding place Edie and I had made ourselves in the cool woods overlooking the river, so that it turned into a game of "Name That Tune" for us. There was a stream of rock 'n' roll: Queen, Steve Miller, ELO, the Eagles. Nell and Josie's voices were lost beneath the blur of music.

My mother arose early and was sometimes joined by Stella, who helped her hoe the garden. Mom paid special attention to her cantaloupes while Stella tended the tomatoes. They worked in silence for long stretches, but would sometimes talk in low tones for a while, too, pausing only to lean on their hoes when either the conversation or the knots of pain in the smalls of their backs grew especially serious.

Every two or three days, a thunderstorm would save us all. The storms gave plenty of warning. First there was a breeze. Then gusts of wind came twitching down the valley, setting the leaves to rock, turning their white sides out. We all stood outside in the wind, breathing in the air before the oncoming rain. We became so caught up in the smell of the approaching downpour—the best, cleanest scent—that often we didn't have time to get inside before the rain simply dropped out of the sky in a sudden pounding. The rain always fell straight down, so hard that it made perfectly round dents in the dust. By the time I had run for cover beneath the screen porch, the rain was falling on the tin roof with a sound like a great drone of Bible insects descending on us. Other times the drops sounded like quarters hitting the roof, and I imagined an old man with a wild mane of white hair leaning out of an airplane to shower the world with change.

One day, just as I was racing up the steps to the porch, Mom and Nell rushed past me the other way, laughing, like I was invisible. They were both barefoot, and their freckled feet looked elegant and white against the muddied yard. As a boom of thunder shook the ground, they stood there and spread their arms out at the same time, as if they had practiced these movements earlier. They twirled and danced, laughing like crazy women, their faces leaning back to catch the rain in their eyes. They looked like young girls to me, their hair soaking wet, their skin smoothed and shined by the water.

"Oh, God," my mother said, two little words of praise. I could barely hear her over the pounding on the tin roof.

Nell twirled around, her arms raised.

I stood near the screen, watching them, the warm mist of rain breathing against my face. Occasionally they touched hands, leaning back so the rain could hit their faces, holding their palms up to catch the drops. I was mesmerized.

The rain never lasted more than ten minutes at the most. This day it lasted even less, and when it was finished, the drops seemed to be sucked right back up into the sky, leaving the world to bake and steam.

Nell shook her head, and drops of water glistened out

from her. She stepped up onto the porch, letting the screen door slam behind her. "Lord, that felt good," she said. She wiped a hand over her face and smiled down at me as if she'd known I was there the whole time. "I've never understood why people run to get out of the rain in the summertime," she said, running her hand through her hair. "People will drive miles and miles to go jump in a cool swimming hole, but when it rains, they scatter." She sloshed on by me, into the house.

Out on the yard, my mother had gone completely still, her back to me. She was facing the woods, where the sounds of rain continued—a deep, hollow music—as the trees dripped. What memory or thought was she caught up in? What secret played out on her face if I could have seen it? Somehow I knew there was regret in her eyes as she faced the dripping woods and listened to the recovering trees. Her shoulders were square with sadness. I thought of calling to her, or even walking out there and taking hold of her hand, but I didn't. I was afraid she wouldn't notice me.

Instead, I kept my place on the porch. Now the garden soil was dark brown and the leaves of Edie's willow seemed brighter, more alive. But already the puddles had been soaked up and the sun had come out again, brighter than before. I closed my eyes for a time and listened to the woods, the melody being pecked out by water dripping onto leaves.

With my eyes closed, I pictured the man Daddy had

killed. I had been having this problem ever since reading that letter, often taking an hour or more to go to sleep at night. I had made up his face in my mind. I saw his fingers uncurl from his rifle, heard the dull thump of his body hitting the ground. Saw my father's face go pale, the cold beads of sweat popping out on his forehead.

I opened my eyes because I didn't want to think about it anymore.

By the time Daddy came home from work, the ground was so parched again that he found me, Nell, and Josie sitting on the grass in the backyard. He leaned down and kissed Josie's cheek, and she didn't even acknowledge him. This was troubling to me; a year ago she would have gotten up to hug him. Once she had always been with him, and now she stood completely apart, avoiding him at all costs. I wondered how this made my father feel, how he could be silent about that. Then again, he was usually silent about everything, which is most likely why he stayed on the edge of explosion all the time. When he did say anything at length, it was sometimes in a rant that came out of nowhere. Daddy ran his hand over my head and stomped on into the house for his shower. Nell paused from her talking long enough to look after him. He hadn't even spoken to her.

Nell was giving us a music lesson.

"If you want to know good music, then all you have to do is listen to the Carter Family, the Beatles, Bob Dylan, and Nina Simone," she said, turning back to us. She took four albums out of a milk crate. The green record player sat near her bare feet. "That's all it takes to have good taste."

She laid the albums out on the grass, like big square playing cards. I looked at the Carter Family album and noted the women's heavy wool coats, the man's stiff suit, their steely gazes into the camera.

"They look madder than fire," I said.

"People didn't smile for cameras back then," Nell said. "They didn't have much to smile about. But they're the best. They're *real*."

"Plus it took so much longer to take a picture," Josie said.

Nell tapped the album cover showing a beautiful black woman in a red dress. "Nina," she said, as if this were someone she knew and missed very much. She held the album by the cover and let the record slide out. "You have to hear this."

She put the needle on the correct groove and sat back with her hands behind her, her eyes closed as the song started. She mouthed the words as the woman sang, *"Ne me quitte pas."*

The song was in French, so neither Josie nor I could understand a word of it, but somehow I could hear the sadness caught in the notes. I liked it, but I wasn't about to admit this. The music floated out to each corner of the yard, tightening the air. Nell shook her head just a bit with the words, the way someone does when they are particularly satisfied. A smile played on her lips, but she looked as she always did when singing, as if she would cry, too. Josie was watching Nell with a strange little smirk on her face, as if she thought Nell was incredibly beautiful or psychotic or maybe both.

When the song ended, with many repetitions of *"Ne me quitte pas,"* the needle caught a couple of specks of dust and crackled out before Nell lifted the arm. She looked as if the song had worn her out. Even though she hadn't shed any tears, her eyes were wet, so she wiped them with the backs of her wrists.

"What does it mean?" I said, quiet, afraid of breaking some kind of grace that had fallen over us.

Nell didn't look at me and didn't speak until she had put the record back in its sleeve. She stared down at the album cover. "It means 'Don't leave me,'" she said.

None of us said anything for a time. The song had caused a great silence to collect in the yard, as if all the usual sounds of evening had retreated into the deepest part of the woods. Nell finally slid the album back into the milk crate.

"I know Bob Dylan's stuff," Josie said proudly. "'Blowin' in the Wind' and all that. He can't sing worth a dime."

"Well, that's the *beauty* of his singing," Nell said, and didn't offer to explain further. She held the Dylan album out to Josie. "Take it and listen to it when you get a chance. Especially 'You're Gonna Make Me Lonesome When You Go.' That one will rip your guts out." She stacked the other albums up and put the record player atop them, then gathered them all up in her arms and stood, her knees popping. "I bet supper is almost ready, and we should've been helping Loretta," she said.

"Wait," Josie said. "What about the Beatles? Which is your favorite song?"

"Oh, God," Nell said, walking away. She stopped after putting one foot on the porch steps and looked back at us, clutching everything to her chest. "Every damn one of them."

"Nell, watch that dirty mouth," said my mother, who was suddenly standing at the screen door. "And y'all come on and eat."

As Mom went back into the house, I saw Daddy standing in the open kitchen door. He had been eavesdropping. His face was solid and straight-edged, the way the sky looks when a storm can blow up out of nowhere.

When Nell opened the screen door and held it so I could go onto the porch, he sank back into the kitchen, never taking his eyes from mine. I had caught him looking at me like this before, and I still couldn't figure out what he saw when he stared like that. I thought that maybe he didn't see anything at all. Instead, he was looking past me, picturing the trees of Vietnam.

"Well, go on, Eli," Nell said with a little laugh in her voice. "You're letting flies in."

I ran across the porch and into the kitchen, where I was

covered up in the smell of fried chicken, biscuits, gravy, and fried apples. I sat down at the table and grabbed up my fork and knife, but Mom said I had to go wash my hands first. As I was getting up, I caught a few muffled words that Nell was saying to Daddy, so I crept near the door frame and listened, even though I knew I shouldn't. To have seen them would have risked their seeing me, but I could hear them just fine.

"And they're sure?" Daddy said, and Nell must have nodded, because he went on: "What can they do?"

"They think they'll have to take them," Nell said. Her voice was quiet and dark, not her voice at all.

"There's no way around it?"

"It's cancer, Stanton. There's nothing else they can do."

I didn't know exactly what Nell meant, but I was smart enough to know that cancer was a very bad thing. I had heard of it killing old people before. As much as I didn't want anything else to agonize about that summer, I tucked it away in my list of other things to worry about when I sat with my beech tree. There was the atom bomb, the Rapture, the possibility that I might be possessed by the devil, the threat that my parents might someday not love each other, or me. And now I could add that Nell had something wrong with her.

If I had known how bad it actually was, that would have been all I would have thought about the rest of that summer.

ELEVEN

I had begged Daddy for weeks to let me go to work with him.

For some reason, that morning he let me sit on his lap and steer the truck, although he kept one thumb hooked on the lower corner of the wheel, to make sure I didn't wreck us. He turned up the radio and tapped his thumb in beat to the song, and I felt as if I were driving all alone, a grown boy in control of the world. After a time he kissed the back of my head, his signal to me to slide off his lap and let him drive the rest of the way. He always said if I drove too far, the cops would get us.

I hadn't been kissed by my father in ages, so after moving, I sat there and looked at him for what seemed a long while before I rolled down my window and let my hand float up and down on the rushing air as the hills and river sped by.

When we came to the high bridge where the little boy had died, Daddy slowed, as if paying respect. I started to ask him what he knew about the dead boy, but there was something about his face that told me to not speak. He was peering over the railing of the bridge, his mouth set in a firm line, his eyes slow to blink. I thought I saw him swallow hard, his Adam's apple rising in a gulp. Maybe he saw the child's ghost and didn't want me to know. His whole body changed — tensed, became bigger, more solid — when we passed over the bridge. But then we were back on the road and he was speeding up again, and it didn't feel right to mention anything. I was having such a fine time that I didn't want to spoil it by bringing up a dead boy. Before long we arrived at the station.

I loved everything about the Ashland station: the smell of oil in the garage, the long black tube that ran across the pavement in front of the gas pumps, the bell that rang when a car drove over this tube, approaching for gas. I admired the way the wide metal shelf had been attached to the ceiling over the cash register. This shelf held brightly colored packs of cigarettes that were gotten to by reaching up and snatching one down. When one pack was removed, another slid down into its place, which struck me as ingenious. I loved the three separate boxes of candy bars that stood on the counter. The orange box for Reese's cups, the brown one for Hershey bars, and the red one that held Zagnuts. There was no store at my father's station, only these boxes of candy, along with the cigarettes, a glass jar that held Blow Pop suckers, and the oil filters, air hoses, and timing belts that hung on the wall behind the counter. There was a Pepsi machine out on the curb in front of the station that ticked especially loud when it was hot, struggling to keep the bottles cold.

My father owned and operated the gas station with only two helpers. One was an older man — called String because he was so tall and skinny — who was an expert at repairing engines. People brought their cars from miles around so he could work on them. String did not say much but always winked at me and produced a stick of Fruit Stripe gum from his shirt pocket, offering it with greasy fingers. Then he'd wink at me again and give his own wad of gum a loud chomp. The other employee was Jack, who had been the valedictorian of his senior class but wanted to work awhile before going to college. My father said that Jack was all book sense and nothing else, since he was dumb as Nixon when it came to practical matters. He tended to smaller jobs like pumping gas, cleaning windshields, rotating tires, plugging flat tires, or changing oil. Any new task had to be explained to him in such great detail that my father usually just gave up and did whatever had to be done himself. Jack was eager to please, though, and was good to me, often talking to me at length about books. That summer I was fairly obsessed with *The Diary of Anne Frank,* which Edie had read the previous winter and had talked about so much that I had to read it to find out what all the fuss was about.

"There's a lot of wisdom to be found in that little book," Jack said after I told him what I was reading. "It's amazing, really, what that little girl wrote. That one line, 'Despite everything, I still believe that people are really good at heart.' That right there, now, I'll just tell you, that'll stand the test of time, buddy."

I hadn't gotten that far into the book yet, so I tried to tune out anything he said lest he spoil the entire plot. On his lunch break he ate a baloney-and-mustard sandwich he had brought from home, drank a Mountain Dew, and immersed himself in a book called *Jude the Obscure,* sitting on a stack of tires in the cool corner of the garage. Once when I asked him what the book was about, he told me it was only the best book ever written and that as soon as I got old enough, I ought to read it, and he was about to go on and on but the bell clanged, drawing my attention to a car that needed to be filled with gas, which was my job when I went along with my father to the station.

The drivers were tickled by the sight of a ten-year-old

pumping their gas (I was too short to clean the windshields or check their oil, so Jack had to run out and do that) and sometimes gave me a quarter tip, which I saved up for the movies. I was hoping to go see *The Bad News Bears,* although my mother said Josie would have to take me since she couldn't stand Walter Matthau. Lots of actors got on my mother's nerves, and she had strong opinions about all of them.

I longed for a shirt like the ones my father, Jack, and String all wore. The shirts were dark blue, heavily starched. The best part was that they all had a little blue-bordered patch over their left pocket that announced their names. I had begged for such a shirt for the last two years but had never received one, always expecting it as a birthday present. Daddy said they didn't make them in my size.

The gas station was situated on the side of the road between our house and Refuge in a space of countryside that had been devoted to a scattering of businesses. On one side of us was a small grocery, and on the other side was a pay-by-the-week motel where a few old bachelors lived year-round. The motel was painted turquoise and had a dry pool in its courtyard. This had once been the main road, before the interstate came through on the other side of town, and my father said that when he was a child, the motel had been considered fancy. People told how Lucille Ball had once stayed there, back in the fifties. On the two occasions I had ventured close to the motel to spy on people, it had smelled of lard and rotting sawdust. The first time I had seen nothing except an old man in Bermuda shorts, black socks, and a gray fedora with a red feather in the band, reading the newspaper as he sat outside his door on one of the plastic patio chairs that came with each room. The second time there had been a group of old men playing poker around a card table they had set up on the courtyard. They smoked and cussed, but that had been the extent of anything interesting.

The other side of the road was taken up by a mile-long cornfield. Beyond that was the river, which was why the cornfield was situated there in the first place, in the rich bottomland. And beyond the river were blue mountains that always seemed striped with jagged lines of heat.

It was especially hot that day, so hot that Jack pointed out to me how the gases shifted and moved over the pavement. He said that it was because of the oils trapped in the blacktop being conjured up by the heat. This was like something my mother would say, since she was always seeing the world through its science, and I thought how she and Jack would probably get along very well.

"Did you have my mother for a teacher in high school?"

"Yeaaaah," he said, in his sly, slow way of dragging out one-syllable words. "She taught me that, about the gases. She was the best teacher I ever had. I always loved English and history, but she made me care about science."

I had heard people say such things about my mother for

as long as I could remember. I thought she was very noble, to be able to make someone love a school subject they hadn't even thought of before.

My father often announced — out of nowhere, for no known reason — that Americans loved their cars even more than they loved their dogs. So I felt running a gas station was pretty important, too. My mother taught people how to do things, and my father took care of things that some people found impossible to learn. And during the oil shortage last year, he had supplied everyone with gas easily, even though we had seen cars lined up in the cities on the evening news.

The best thing about the gas station, however, was that my father was a different person there. Somehow he was more relaxed there than at home. Our house, and my world, was always covered up in women. My mother, Nell, Josie, Stella, Edie. Those five were such big presences that a couple of them alone would have been overpowering enough. But here, at the Ashland station, my father was in a man's world, and one he knew inside out. I wondered if being here reminded him of the good parts of being at war, the way men are able to trust one another and become close in ways they might not under normal circumstances. I also saw that while my father was mostly at a loss for expertise at home — often being called on only to be the middleman between Mom and Josie's fights, or some such thing — here he was always in control. At the station he knew the answer to everything. People didn't question him. They looked up to him. Of course we looked up to him at home, too, but usually with a seed of doubt in our throats. He was not very good at explaining himself, and we were a family that liked to have things clearly laid out for us. At the station, he and his small crew had a sort of shorthand. He could holler out a line of numbers and String would magically appear, producing a particular brake pad or oil filter.

Daddy tried to show me things, to teach me how to change a tire or simply glance at a shiny row of sockets and know which size I needed for the job at hand. He sometimes put his oily hand atop mine to direct me in the correct way to tighten or loosen a bolt or nut. He looked me in the eye. And most of all, he talked to me. He talked to me more during one day at work together than he would have during an entire week at home.

Still, the women made it clearly known what they wanted me to do at home, and he did not. He was vague with his demands, and there were rarely second chances. My father did not like to explain himself twice and expected me to learn how to do something after one discussion. Here I felt the need to impress and often failed. He also cussed here occasionally, which my mother would have frowned upon. She said while cussing might not send you to hell, it would make people think you were rude. When he let loose a bad word, he'd wink at me as if this was our secret. There seemed to be an understanding between us that I was not to

cuss until I became a man. Only then would it be accept-
able, and even then it was preferable to do this only in front
of other men.

During our lunch break, I read my book while we ate.
My mother had packed our lunch. A ham-and-cheese sandwich for my father and peanut-butter-and-jelly for me. She
had wrapped some Pringles up in aluminum foil for me.
Daddy got us each a Zagnut bar off the counter and bought
us each our own bottle of Pepsi from the machine. We sat
on tires in the back corner of the garage, where it was cool
and shadowy.

"Do you have to read that old book even while you're
eating?" he said, chewing a couple of my chips.

"It's so good I can't hardly lay it down."

"Well, reading's good," he said. "But learning how to
fix a motor will come in handier for you."

"It's about this little girl who had to hide from the
Nazis."

He stopped chewing, offended, and looked at me for a
silent moment. "I know who Anne Frank is," he said, his
whole face tightening. "Do you think I'm an idiot?"

I marked my place with a postcard of the Lincoln
Memorial that Nell had sent me a year ago, and laid the
book aside.

It was so hot we could hear the cicadas — my father
called them heat bugs — screaming even over the dirty little
radio sitting atop a huge red toolbox. When "The Most

Beautiful Girl" came on, my father sang along very loud while he changed tires or installed air filters. It was no wonder we could hear the insects mourning the heat, though, because my father never turned the radio up very loud. He said the customers didn't like to pull in and be blasted away.

The thunderstorms usually rolled in later in the evening, just before dusk, but that day we had just finished our lunch break when the sky fell open. Daddy was in the garage, lying on the wooden rolling bed that enabled him to scoot up under cars, checking an oil leak on an El Camino. String had half his body hanging out of the engine of a Charger, which was also pulled into one of the bays of the garage. Jack had nothing else to do except sweep cigarette butts off the concrete slab that served as a small porch. Very few cars had come along lately, so I had settled in on the pile of tires to read my Anne Frank book. I was just to the part where Anne kissed Peter when we felt the air change. Then the low rumble of thunder. A warning, a music.

Jack looked up at the sky. "Man, it's going to be a bad one," he said, and pointed to the horizon over the far hills. "Look — those clouds are almost green, they're so full."

I ran in and put my book on the counter so it wouldn't get wet, then came back out to see the rain moving toward us through the corn. The storm churned in like a moving wall. The tops of the corn trembled in the downpour, and a boom of thunder made the ground shudder. I looked down, expecting to see the concrete of the slab cracked open, but it wasn't. The cloud chamber paused as the rain thrashed the road in great, round plops, so hard that the rain looked like it was falling backward, rising up out of the blacktop and sizzling skyward.

"That's ozone," Jack said, as if transfixed. "That smell."

Then the storm moved forward and hit the station like an ocean wave. Jack stood on the porch, broom in hand, and flattened himself against the plate-glass window behind him, but I ran out to the gas pumps. I stomped over the hose, but its bell was lost to the sound of pummeling rain and crashing thunder.

I was drenched within seconds, the rain falling so hard that I could barely see as it flowed over my brow and down into my eyes. But I felt like I was leaving my own body, as if I were giving myself up to the storm as I turned in the rain, my arms extended, my face tilted back to receive the water, just as Mom and Nell had done.

I heard my father calling my name — a muted, dulled sound, as if he were on the other side of a waterfall — and through the rain I could see him and String standing in the shelter of the open garage, looking out at me as if I had lost my mind. Lightning flashed between us, a huge whiteness. His mouth opened again, his face gathered in anger, but all sound was lost. Jack still stood on the porch, laughing with both hands perched on the top of the broom, the way my mother sometimes stood in the garden with her hoe when she was looking around for any missed weeds.

I closed my eyes again, turned, and gave myself over to the thunderstorm. I imagined I was standing on the bottom of a fast-moving river that churned around me. And then my father's hands were on me and his voice was loud in my ear, a great roar that was too distorted for me to understand. He scooped me up and ran back into the garage with me bobbing on his hip.

Once there, he half threw me down but I landed on my feet. I looked up at him, feeling his anger wash over me. He trembled before me, his eyes furious, full of the war. I had gotten old enough to identify it, just like my mother could. Both of us knew when the war had taken control of him. He put his hand out as if to slap me, and I flinched back, waiting for the blow, even though he had never struck me in the face before. When he got mad like this over the most unexpected thing, everything about him changed: the shape of his face, the way he held his body. His hand shook there in front of me as if he was struggling to control it, but then he pulled it back, hard, and shoved it into the pocket of his work pants. He looked down, shook his head. No one spoke. A wall of thunder shook the ground. Just when I thought he was going to walk away, Daddy bent at the waist and grabbed me by both arms, shaking me.

"Why did you do that? What's wrong with you?"

"Puh-leez-duh-on't-Da-ddy," I said, feeling as if he were shaking my teeth out of my skull.

"Have you lost your mind?" Daddy boomed, his eyes wild, his grip tightening on my arms. "That lightning was running all across that blacktop. Could've killed you."

Out of the corner of my eye, I saw String step forward as if to intervene, but before he could, Daddy stopped. He squatted down so that we were eye level, wiping water off my face. I breathed hard and rain slid into the corners of my mouth, washing down my cheeks. My feet felt heavy in my wet Chuck Taylors, and my cutoffs stuck to my thighs. I pulled my T-shirt out from my belly and found that it sucked at my skin.

"Why did you do that, Eli?" Daddy asked, calmer now, but still not right, not himself.

"Mom and Nell stood in the storm the other day," I said.

He fretted his eyebrows as if he didn't understand. I thought he might continue to yell at me, but then he held his hand up to my cheek and ran one thumb across the bottom of my chin. He had never touched me so tenderly before. "You scared me to death, little man."

The rain stopped, instantly, as if turned off by a switch on the wall, and the blacktop began to steam, mists rising and snaking through the corn. The bruised clouds cleared like a curtain snatched away to reveal white clouds against a blinding sky.

Daddy was still squatting there before me, looking up at my face as if he hadn't seen me in ages. And then I saw that he wasn't there, really. He wasn't behind his own eyes.

I didn't know what was scarier to me: when he looked me dead in the eye, hollering, or when he turned away and was quiet. Lately everything about him was terrifying to me. I felt all the time like my nerves would shoot out of the tips of my fingers.

"It's all right, Stanton," String said, standing behind Daddy. String took another step toward my father, then stopped, as if he knew better than to get too close. "Come on, now, buddy."

Daddy rose as if pulling up a great load and moved past me, going in the side door that connected with the room where the cash register stood on the counter. He shrugged through the doorway and into the register room. The door had two glass panels, so I could see him in there, leaning on the counter near the register with one hand, staring at the back wall. His face was dry, but his body held the language of defeat and maybe even weeping: his shoulders arched, his head shook back and forth.

String didn't walk away, as I thought he might, but pulled a piece of Fruit Stripe from his pocket. "Here ye go, buddy," he said.

"Why'd he get so mad?"

"One of his friends got struck by lightning over there in Vietnam," String said in his slow, easy way. "They was walking across a big rice field, knee deep in water. Didn't you know that, squirt?"

"No," I said, and put the orange gum into my mouth. "He never talks about the war."

String dipped his fingers into the tub of hand cleanser sitting atop the tire changer and soaped up. "Yeah, he don't talk much about it, for sure," he said. His face was so lined by weather and life that some of the furrows seemed like knife scars. "But every once in a while, he'll tell a little something if you listen real close."

"I listen all the time. To everything."

"Well," String said, and went back to the Charger and peered in at the engine. "Listen some more."

A car pulled in and the bell rang, announcing its entrance. It was Charles Asher and Josie in his fine Mustang. I walked out to them slowly, this new weight of knowledge slowing me down, and before I could even speak to them, Jack stepped down off the porch and tousled my wet hair. "You're a sight, man," he said.

Daddy told me to go on home with Josie and Charles Asher since I was soaked and would be of no use to his customers if I looked like a drowned rat. He had stayed by the register a few minutes before coming out to greet Josie and Charles Asher.

On the drive home, I sat on the edge of the backseat so I

could prop my chin right behind Josie's head. She sat close to Charles Asher and didn't turn to say anything to me. Instead, she looked through the rearview mirror when she questioned me about why I was so wet, what had happened during my day, what Jack was up to. Everybody in the family was always giving her grief about her inquiries on Jack. I knew, as they all did, that she had a secret crush on him, but he was nineteen and not at all interested in her. Besides, I would have died if she had ever broken up with Charles Asher.

Eventually all conversation ended when the Spinners came on the radio. Josie turned it up and moved around in her seat a bit, singing every word. She was in a good mood today, which was unusual for her these days.

"Hey, y'all prepare yourself for the Rubberband Man," she sang. This song made absolutely no sense to me, but it had a good beat, so I scooted back against the seat and sang, too, watching as the hills and houses rushed by, the river coming up next to the road as we neared our house. But I stopped singing, weighted down by the fact that I had once again been sent off to be with the women.

I wondered if my father had really had me go with Josie because I was wet or if he had sent me away because he was ashamed of me.

The music and Josie's singing and the sound of the rushing wind coming through the open windows and everything else faded away from me. And then I was all alone, sitting in the backseat of some unmanned car racing down the highway. There was nothing but the road and the hills and the river. I'm not sure if they were ghosts or my imagination — I still don't know — but when I looked down to the riverbank, I could see a line of soldiers, their machine guns held out in front of them as they moved cautiously through the water toward some uncertain death. Or maybe even life.

TWELVE

My mother snapped a pillowcase out onto the hot, still air. "Why are you wet?" she asked. It was so hot that my hair and shirt had already dried, but my denim shorts were still heavy with rain.

She listened as I answered, standing at the clothesline, a full basket of sheets at her feet. One fitted sheet had already been latched to the line, so that our backyard had been over-taken by the scent of detergent and Downy.

"Well, are those wet shorts rubbing your legs raw?" she asked, and pinned the pillowcase to the line. Apparently she didn't think my dancing in the rain was particularly strange, or interesting.

I shook my head no.

"Then stay outside and play. You'll dry soon, hot as it is. I've got enough clothes to wash without adding more to the pile."

I ran away across the yard before she could think of something else for me to do besides play. As I scampered away, I heard Mom tell Josie and Charles Asher to go help Nell break up beans. Josie responded with an exaggerated sigh, but Charles Asher said "Yes, ma'am," in his polite way that didn't seem so much like brown nosing as actual respect.

The midday rain had only made the day hotter. The air seemed like a solid thing.

I went to Edie's and pounded on the back door, but nobody answered. An empty bottle of Dr Pepper stood in a wet ring on the small table by the door and Edie's copy of *The Outsiders* lay on the porch swing, so she couldn't have been gone long. She was on her third reading of this book, as she said it was her favorite of all time, and I opened it to find places I had seen her marking with a red ink pen. On the first page she had scrawled "loneliness" and then, farther down the margin, she had written, "He's different." I laid the paperback down where I had found it, sure that Edie would punch me for having looked at her thoughts, and went around to her bedroom window and peered in. The shades were drawn to keep the heat out, but when I pecked on the window frame, there was no answer, either. This was unusual, as Edie usually chose to stay home alone even when her parents went somewhere.

I let the screen door to our porch slam behind me and found Nell sitting in her usual place on the glider. A newspaper was spread across her lap to catch the strings she peeled away from the green beans. She tossed the broken beans into a bowl that had been placed on the floor. Josie and Charles Asher had pulled the rockers up close to the bowl. Josie looked put out by this chore, but Charles Asher was happy, as usual. He broke the beans carefully, but Josie snapped them in a hard-rhythmed blur.

Nell looked up when the door slammed, a smile playing on her lips. "Here he is, Mother Nature's son," she said.

"What's that mean?" I said, on the defense.

"You stood in the rain, didn't you?" Nell said, turning her eyes back to her hands, where she expertly broke the beans in four singular pops. I was surprised by how effortlessly she went about this kind of work. She looked much more herself with a book in her hands. "In the storm?"

"Yeah," I said. "You were right. It did feel good."

"I told you," she said. She smiled at the beans in her lap. "You're always reminding me of that Beatles song, the way you spend so much time in the woods, and the river. And now standing in thunderstorms."

"What song?"

Only then did her hands become still. She paused for just a moment, her fingers hovering over the pile of unbroken beans that lay spread out across the newspaper, mixed in with her discarded strings.

"You haven't heard 'Mother Nature's Son'?" she asked, completely taken aback. When I said no, she looked out to where my mother was finishing up hanging the sheets on the line. "Loretta, have you deprived these children of the Beatles?"

"What?" my mother called, plucking a clothespin from her mouth.

"Nothing!" Nell hollered back, loud. Then, to me: "I'll play it for you later on. You have to hear it."

"Where's Edie at, Eli?" Josie asked. She had a teasing smile on her face, as if she was so mad about having to break beans that she wanted to take it out on me.

I shrugged. "I don't know."

"You don't know where Edie is?" she gasped, acting shocked. She laughed at herself. "That's a first."

"I'm not her keeper," I said. I had heard Josie say this many times about me, when I was hidden somewhere and my mother asked her where I was. I didn't exactly know what this phrase meant, but it made sense somehow.

"You don't know where your *girl*friend is?"

"Shut up, Josie," I said. It wasn't often that we fought, but when we did, the arguments were usually brutal screaming matches. Josie reserved all her kindness for me, it seemed, but when she was feeling especially cruel, she took pity on no one.

"Josie," Nell scolded, but there was laughter in her voice. "You *love* her," she singsonged. "You want to *marry* her."

"Shut up!" I yelled.

"Josie," Charles Asher said, quiet. "Leave him alone, now."

Josie laughed, a high, clear sound I couldn't help appreciating, even though I was furious at her. Her laugh would save her many, many times in her life. There was no denying its beauty. "I was just kidding you, little man," she said, but I got up and stormed away, letting the screen door slam behind me again. "Don't be that way, now," she called to me as I ran away. The thing that made me most angry about Josie was that I found it nearly impossible to be mad at her. She always did something like let loose of that great laugh or put just enough love into the way she called me little man, and I forgave her completely. It was a curse.

So I went to the snowball bush.

When my father returned from Vietnam, my mother had planted a snowball bush in the side yard to commemorate his survival. The bush had grown unnaturally big and by the summer of 1976 was as big as a small shed and so roomy that it served as a perfect playhouse for Edie and me. Inside, the branches made room for two little chairs we had dragged in there. The ground was hard, packed dirt. In

June the blossoms were in full bloom, so often the floor of our playhouse was littered with white petals that looked like identical pieces of waxy confetti. The snowball bush didn't have a particularly overpowering scent except in the early mornings, when the whole place smelled of vanilla.

Our family spent most of our time on the screen porch, which was out back. When people used the front porch, they usually were seeking privacy, so that the juiciest and most shocking conversations often took place there. The front porch was mostly used by Josie, since she was on constant lookout for privacy. Sometimes she would run the long yellow phone cord across the living room and out the front door, close the door, and then prop herself up on one of the porch chairs to have a long conversation with one of her girlfriends. It was also Josie's habit to direct Charles Asher out to the front porch. People rarely passed on our road, except in the mornings and evenings, when they were either going to or coming from work, so hardly anyone would see them there. But you never knew who might show up at the back of our house. People were always walking across a succession of backyards to reach our place and congregate on our screen porch. Stella burst in unannounced all the time, as did Edie and various others. Nell had pretty much taken possession of the screen porch since her arrival, too, so any privacy that had once been found there was completely gone now, as there was hardly any time when Nell wasn't out there smoking or reading or gazing out at the garden as if all the secrets to life were hidden beneath the damp petals of cucumber vines.

Edie and I had a few select toys we left in three tin boxes beneath the snowball bush. One box held a collection of silver and blue jacks, along with a raggedy deck of cards. Edie had taught me to play rummy, and even though she always beat me, I still loved to play there in the hidden world where nobody could see her get the better of me. In another tin there were several colored pencils (last summer we had left crayons out here but despite the shade they had still melted into one multicolored, square clump that we spent the rest of the summer prying out with my pocketknife) and a small pad of paper.

In the other tin was our entire collection of plastic cowboys, which were blue or orange; Indians, some yellow and some red; and soldiers, which were all green. We had outgrown them but I actually missed playing with them, so I chose them to entertain me until Josie and Charles Asher made their way out onto the front porch. I was sure this would happen before long; my sister was predictable in most matters.

I lined all the soldiers up in one line, clumped the cowboys on a small hill I formed by raking dirt into a pile, then took two fingers to dig out a wide trench where the Indians waited in hiding.

I made shooting sounds by pursing my lips and blowing

out air, raked all the cowboys down, flicked the soldiers over one by one by using thumb and forefinger the way Nell sent cigarettes flying across the yard when she was finished with them. Then I ran each Indian up the hill and had them dance over the slaughtered masses. I always let the Indians win. I don't know why.

Josie and Charles Asher made their way out onto the front porch and the chains of the porch swing clinked when they sat down. Josie kicked at the floor with a bare foot to get them swinging. She put her right leg up over both of his and then a hand up to his face and drew him into her lips. Soft kisses at first, then her head moved around the way necking couples did in the movies. She chewed at his lips, arching her body in toward his, although they were sitting in an awkward position, being on the swing together. He sat very stiff and ran his hand up her back until his fingers disappeared beneath her hair. I imagined this to be a cool place, in the shade. Like the space beneath the snowball bush.

Josie put her hand on Charles Asher's chest and slid two fingers in between the buttonholes on his madras shirt, and with her other hand she held on to one side of his face, holding him as close as she could. I nearly gagged when I caught a brief glimpse of their tongues knocking at each other. I couldn't understand how this was at all pleasurable, but I recognized the hunger in Josie's tightly closed eyes, in the way she kept digging her leg into his.

But then Charles Asher pulled away, turning his head from her, and put a hand up to his mouth.

"You bit me," he said, as if amazed. He ran a forefinger over his lip, checking for blood.

Josie got up, and halfway through the front door she said, "I'll be right back."

While she was gone, Charles Asher again ran a forefinger over his lip, then held his hand out in front of him. I couldn't see if there was any blood or not, but he kept putting his lips together as if they were numb and he was trying to get the feeling back.

Josie came back out, one hand up under her shirt. She pulled her hand out and I saw that she was holding the small bottle of Jim Beam that she kept in her hiding place. She offered the whiskey to Charles Asher, but when he wouldn't take the bottle, she unscrewed the cap. Standing there before him with her feet planted apart on the porch, she tipped her head back and took a drink like an expert. She brought the pint down, wiped her mouth on the back of her hand, and widened her eyes to show him she was wild and crazy.

"Put that away," Charles Asher said in a loud, angry whisper. "Loretta'll catch us."

"No, she won't," Josie said, and sat down heavily on the swing, causing the chains to pop and screech. "Here, take a drink," she said, handing the bottle to him. He wouldn't.

"I don't want to," he said, looking around the yard to

make sure no one was close by. "I'm not going to do that at your parents' house."

"Goody Two-Shoes," she said, and took another drink. He grabbed the bottle and pulled it away from her mouth, causing a few amber beads to fall out onto her shirt.

"God, now I'll smell like an alcoholic," she said, wiping at the splotch of brown dots. A moment of silence passed between them before she put the cap back on the bottle and laid it between them on the swing.

"Why do you want to act that way, Josie?" he said. "Drinking and always biting everyone's head off and being mad all the time. What's wrong with you?"

"What's wrong with *you*, Charles Asher?" she said, and scooted away from him, close to the arm of the swing. "I've never seen a boy who wouldn't do *any*thing. This is never going to last if you keep right on boring the mortal hell out of me."

Charles Asher shook his head. He looked weary, beaten. "I wish you'd answer me." And then: "What are you so mad about?"

"I just want to have some fun," she said.

"No, it's like you want to get caught with that liquor so you'll get in trouble," he said. "Just like with them flag pants. I believe you want to wear them just to make Loretta mad. You act like you're making a statement with them, but you're not. You're just stirring up —"

"Whose side are you on?" she said, scowling at him.

"I didn't know there were sides," he said. "But I'm getting tired of you treating everybody bad and acting like something you're not. I love you, Josie, but you're turning into a different person from who I first loved."

Josie looked away from him. Up until this point she had kept her eyes on his, but now she turned her face to the wall of the house as if she couldn't bear the sight of him. "You don't know anything about love," she said. "You don't know what it means."

"If anyone don't know, then it's you," he said. "You've got a good family and you're beautiful and you've got anything a person could want and you just stay mad all the time lately."

"How would you feel if you all at once found out you didn't belong to your father?" she said, turning to him. It took me a long time of looking back on that evening to realize that by finally making this known to someone else she had freed herself in a small way. And so that was the beginning of my sister healing. But at that time it was also when the fire of her anger was burning the brightest. That showed in her eyes, too.

So she does know, I thought. A pang of grief for her ran all through me. And then I realized that it really was true. I had read this in Daddy's letters, had overheard Mom talk about it to Stella, but until that moment of hearing Josie say this thing, I hadn't really believed it. I had tried to deny it to myself, I guess. Or maybe it was just that learning my sister was only my half sister didn't matter to me because it didn't change anything. I loved her just the same, and so I understood that Daddy did, too.

"Well?" she said. "Does that surprise you, that my mother got knocked up by somebody else and then Daddy married her, knowing that? That he raised me as his own and nobody told me a damn thing until I was grown?"

"Why did they finally tell you?"

"*Why?* Because I had a right to know, that's why. That's what they said. They sat me down and told me and expected me to just say okay and go on with my life. But I've been lied to all these years. Why didn't they tell me before, when I was little?"

Charles Asher put his arm around her and she laid her head on his shoulder, her hair falling down in her face like a straight, shining curtain of black. "I'm sorry, Josie," he said. "But Stanton worships you. Just because he's not your blood father don't mean he loves you any less. Anybody can see that, man."

Josie put her hands up to her face and her shoulders began to tremble. "I know," she said, her voice hoarse. "But it's killing me." She was trying her best not to cry, but now she was and there was no turning back. She was finally letting it out. "It's my history," she said.

It felt like I should do something, but I didn't know what to do, so I just stood there and tried to not look at them for a while. I don't know what my worst crimes were that summer — the times that I didn't do enough or the times I did too much. I've studied on it for years and can't arrive at the answer.

Charles Asher was trying his best to comfort her — kissing the top of her head, rolling the ball of her shoulder around in his hand, whispering into her ear — but there was nothing he could do to make her feel better, and he knew this. His face was pale and blank, like a piece of unlined notebook paper. But he was off the hook before long because the real Josie returned. The Josie who believed in being strong and defiant.

She straightened herself. Ran her long fingers over her face, then through her hair, and then wiped her nose with the back of her hand. She got up from the swing and stood in front of Charles Asher with her back to me, her fingers slid into the back pockets of her bell-bottoms. "You're a good guy, Charles Asher," she said. "You're *too* good. It drives me frigging crazy."

"Well, I don't know what to do about that," he said. There was no joking in all this. They were being completely honest, which people rarely do with one another.

"Come on, let's go see if supper's ready," she said. And just like that she had shed all her tears and made this secret a solid sentence that had actually floated out onto the air.

And she'd be all right, I guess. But not before it all exploded properly. That's how Josie was.

They went into the house and the yard was quiet again. Even though there was no one to hide from, I crawled back to the snowball bush and lay on the cool ground. I looked at the white petals above me, listened to the running river, and wished that I were grown.

THIRTEEN

I sat on the orange-and-yellow linoleum of the kitchen floor after dinner, playing with my Hot Wheels and my Muhammad Ali action figure, which I was careful to not call a doll, while Nell and Mom and Josie washed the dishes. They discussed everything from the Yablonski murder trials to Jimmy Carter's teeth to why Josie never had any girlfriends over to the house.

"I can't stand to be around them for more than ten minutes," Josie was saying. "They're all idiots."

"Why do you hang around with them, then?" Mom asked, wiping down the counter.

"Because *every*body's an idiot," Josie said. "If I didn't hang out with them, there'd be nobody."

"What makes them idiots, though?" This from Nell.

"They all love Leif Garrett and the Bay City Rollers, for instance. *None* of them thinks Steve McQueen is beautiful," she said. She kept her eyes on the plate she was scrubbing clean. "They're just annoying."

"What matters is whether they're a good friend or not," Mom said. She took the plate from Josie and rubbed at it with her dishrag so that little squeaks pecked at the air.

"What matters is when you don't want to sit around and stare at posters of David Cassidy and talk about how *dreamy* he is for hours on end."

Nell laughed. "Well, who needs them, anyhow? You have all of us, and books, and records. That's all anyone needs."

Dirty plates slid into the warm water and emerged shiny and dripping. Their lemon smell filled the kitchen and drifted out to the backyard, where Daddy was whittling with a Case knife and Charles Asher was looking out on the yard. Watching lightning bugs, I suspected. When the women came out, Daddy and Charles Asher carried chairs down from the screen porch and sat them up in a circle near the clothesline, on the cooling yard. After an especially hot day, the smells of the baking woods were stout. I could smell every single leaf, every blackberry that was beginning to lengthen on the vines behind the garden, every tomato and cucumber. I breathed in everything.

Over at Edie's house the windows were still unlit. I couldn't figure out where in the world she had gone off to without telling me. Edie didn't do anything without informing me first, so I figured her parents had just jerked her up unexpectedly and taken off somewhere. Maybe they had finally worked everything out and had gone off to celebrate. I didn't know.

I decided to wander around by myself in the darker parts of the yard, catching lightning bugs. Then I heard some boys letting out high laughs down by the river and knew that it was Paul and Matt flying by on the road. I could hear them pedaling, faster and faster. Just when they got in front of my house, Matt started counting—"One, two, three"—and then they shouted in unison: "Loooooooser!" They fell apart laughing and pedaled on. I knew this had been directed at me, and my first reaction was to not care, but some part of me did, I guess. Something in me hurt, even though I didn't want it to.

One of the reasons I had stopped playing with Paul and Matt was actually because of an argument we had had over lightning bugs. They always wanted to pull the glowing part off the bugs and smear it onto our faces so that we looked as if we were wearing glow-in-the-dark paints. They also liked to keep the bugs in Mason jars until they had smothered to death. I thought that both options of play were wrong. I saw no use in killing something just for the sake of a few minutes' fun. Of course I had been deemed a sissy because of this, and I was glad they didn't come around anymore. Once school started back, I'd have to face them every day on the bus, but for now it was still summer, and I was free of them.

Instead of murdering or imprisoning the lightning bugs, I liked to cup them in my hand, unfold my fingers, let them walk around on my knuckles until they got ready to leave, and then — my favorite part — watch them take flight again. Seeing something put out wings and sail away was much more satisfying than mashing it between your fingers or stomping it with your shoe. Paul and Matt thought this was nonsense and stopped coming. And I didn't even care.

I was letting one of the lightning bugs tremble away from my outstretched finger when I realized that Nell was hovering very close by, partially hidden behind the snowball bush, watching me. I could see her out of the corner of my eye, but for a long while I didn't let on that I knew she was there. She was standing with one hand balled into a fist on her hip and the other clutching a tall glass of sweet tea. She was looking at me as if memorizing me, as if trying to save this moment for some time in the future when she might need to pull it back out for further inspection. I thought of her cancer, and wanted to ask her if *that* was why she looked at me so strangely sometimes. But I didn't have the words for that. When the bug was gone, I twirled on one heel and let out a high "Ha!" to let Nell know she had been caught spying on me.

A smile covered her face, but she still looked mesmerized. "You are the king of this whole big yard," she said. "What kind of king name should we give you?"

"I don't know. Eli the Great, I guess," I said. This sounded fine to me.

"No, I never did like those kings that had 'the Great' at the ends of their name." Nell curled her arm up so that the glass of tea rested against her chest, the ice clinking. "That always meant they had killed the most wives or fought the most wars or something." She kept looking at me, as if the name would spell itself out above my head in lightning bug–lit letters if she waited long enough. She tapped her pointing finger against the glass of tea. "How about Eli the Good? The kings that were called 'the Good' were always kind. They were always good to their people." She nodded firmly, satisfied. She had talked herself into it. "Yes, sir, that's it. That's who you are. Eli the Good, king of his backyard."

"I like it," I said, and nodded. It would be years before I realized — out of the blue — that Nell had heard the boys calling me a loser and had said this to make me feel better. But I choose to believe that she really meant it, too.

"Your daddy's fixing to play his guitar," Nell said, and held out her hand. "Come on."

We rushed around to the back, where everyone was sitting. Daddy was tuning the guitar, which I coveted. I wasn't allowed to touch it, as it was a great treasure. His mother had left him the orange-and-black Gibson. There was mother-of-pearl trim and silver tuning knobs and a deep hollow sound that resonated for a full minute after one of the strings was strummed.

Daddy didn't often play the guitar. My mother was always begging him to, but usually he would just say he didn't feel like it. Apparently he had once played all the time, especially when they first got married. But he never played much after he got back from Vietnam. I hadn't heard him play more than five times in my life, and it was always like this, completely unexpected. I had no idea why he chose certain nights to play again, but I figured it was when he was in an especially good mood. That's the way my father was: either in an especially good mood or a very bad mood. There was seldom any middle ground.

He strummed the Gibson, then plucked each string individually as he tuned the guitar. "Now, what should I play?" he asked, and looked around at each of us in that shy way he only had when he was about to sing.

"How about some Everly Brothers?" Mom said.

"Lord, I can't remember any of them," Daddy said.

My mother put a finger to her mouth and thought hard. She was excited about this. "How about 'Keep on the Sunny Side'?"

"Naw. Let's see," Daddy said, and picked a few notes. Then he seemed to light on a song he wanted to play and nodded, then put his whole hand atop the strings to silence them. "I used to play this one for you all the time when you's little, Josie," he said, and then he started in on "You Are My Flower." There was a full moon, but his face was lost to the shadows when he looked down at the guitar. I imagined that he closed his eyes while he sang.

"You are my flower, that's blooming in the mountain for me," he sang.

I studied Josie. I don't see how she could ever doubt he loved her after he sang that song for her. Daddy was pouring everything right out on the yard for everyone to see. He must have known how she was trying to work her way through all this after they had told her the truth. So this was a gift he was giving her tonight. He was her father, and the blood didn't even matter. Since that night I have come to understand that sometimes the best families of all are those that we create ourselves, the people we choose to be with. But that night I mostly thought about the way Josie was allowing Charles Asher to put his arm around her shoulders even though she rarely held his hand or made any kind of contact with him when our parents were present. Their lawn chairs were pulled up close together.

My mother closed her eyes and mouthed the words to this song; despite her being quiet about it, I could still hear some hints of sadness in the few words she sang aloud.

Nell was smoking and staring at Daddy while he played. Her whole heart was laid bare there on her face as she watched him. I could see how much she admired him, despite their differences. And I could tell how badly she wanted to say all of that to him but could never find the words. She tapped her right foot to the beat of the song.

When Daddy was finished, everyone clapped wildly.

"Wow, I had no idea you could play like that," Charles Asher said, amazed.

Josie looked like she had just seen a ghost. I thought maybe the song was so full of the way he felt about her that she couldn't make her mind work around it, considering what she had recently been told.

"After he went off to Vietnam, I had the hardest time getting you to sleep," Mom said, her voice so sudden and loud on the stillness that we all started, as if we had forgotten she was there. "You'd cry and go on, and then I realized it was because you missed your daddy singing that old song to you."

"So then she'd play that record for you every night," Nell said.

"And me and Nell and your mamaw would sing along with the record, and you'd finally go to sleep," Mom said.

Josie looked embarrassed because her eyes were wet.

"Well, now you need to do one for old Eli," Nell said, leaning forward in her seat and winking at me. "Can you play 'Mother Nature's Son'? I've been telling him about that song."

Daddy raised his eyebrows and let out a loud breath. "I don't know. That's a complicated one, and I've not played it in forever."

"But you used to love that song, remember?" Nell said. Each of her words came out in puffs of blue smoke on the night. "A couple years after you got back from the war, you played it for me one night. You remember that?"

"Yeah," Daddy said in a hushed voice. There was something in the way they looked at each other that made me know this had been an important night in their relationship. I wondered if this had been some quell in the storm that was always brewing between them. Every few years they'd grow back into brother and sister, and then a fight would conjure up out of nowhere, like an unexpected thunderhead, and they'd go without speaking for a few months before making up. It seemed that the last time he had played this song in her presence, things had been momentarily good between them. I admired the way they were able to forgive each other, even if the peace treaties didn't last long.

And then his long fingers were picking out a melody that sounded to me like a bird taking flight, or waves rising and falling on a dark river. He swayed a little in his wooden chair and tapped his foot, becoming some boy I had never known or seen before. "Will you sing it, Nell?" he asked as he played the introduction.

She nodded, flicking her cigarette out across the yard. I watched its red ember sizzle through the air and dim among the grass where it fell. Daddy played more, a long peaking melody. His shoulders were moving now, his head bobbing to the beat. And then Nell started singing.

"Born a poor young country boy, Mother Nature's son," she sang. The sound of her voice spread through me. Hearing her sing felt like warming up after being very cold. Nell's face was fierce and hard in a beautiful way, and didn't match her voice at all, which was high and moved through the air like a slender thread of smoke. Nell didn't close her eyes when she sang this song. Instead, she looked around at each of us with her eyes larger than I'd ever seen them before. She laid her hands — palms up, barely open — atop her legs, and her voice drifted out over the yard and up the ridge, probably to the at-attention ears of the little fox I always imagined watching me, up to the silenced night birds sitting on their chosen tree limbs. She looked at me the longest.

Eventually she began a kind of nonsense chorus that somehow made perfect sense, where she sang, *"Duht duht dah da da da duht duht duht duht dah."* Daddy's picking matched her words perfectly, his fingers completely focused on making each note work. And on this chorus my mother joined in, so that I caught a glimpse of how she and Nell and my father had all been when they first met, when they were young and free and had only their unknown expectations of what their lives would become.

On the last line, Nell's voice went very high, and then her face and body went back to their normal ways, as if some possessing spirit had sizzled out of her body to float about the world again, waiting for someone else to light upon.

When Nell was finished, everyone clapped again, but quiet this time, as if afraid of breaking the mood. We all knew we had seen my father and his sister come together for a few minutes. And we hadn't seen that in a long time.

Nell put a hand to her throat and laughed with some amount of embarrassment or modesty and immediately tapped a cigarette out of her pack. She put it into the corner of her mouth and lit the Winston with a squinted eye, speaking after she drew in the smoke. "See there, Eli? That's your song now, buddy," she said, and brought the Zippo down in a sharp strike against her leg so that the lid snapped shut. "It's just like you."

I nodded. I didn't know what to say, but I did want to claim the song as my own. I wanted it to be a part of me.

"That's my favorite song by them," Nell said.

"Yeah, the Beatles were a great band until they started all that psychedelic stuff and Lennon got on that antiwar kick."

Nell moved around in her seat as if trying to find a comfortable spot, and a look passed between her and my mother. I knew that look, the one my mother gave. It meant: *Be quiet. Hold your tongue.* She had glared at me exactly like that many times.

Nell didn't possess the ability to let things go, though. To her that would have been a sin, a selling of her own self. "Are you directing that towards me, Stanton Book?"

"Take it however you want it. You were the big-time war protester. You marched through New York City and wound up in a history book. I fought an actual war and nobody ever so much as thanked me."

"I marched for *you,*" she said.

"That's such horseshit," Daddy spat, his war face suddenly there, all at once, without warning. He wouldn't look at her. "And you know it," he added.

"Stanton," my mother said, her chiding voice.

"What did you expect me to do, Stanton? Set here and keep praying for you? That war wasn't right and you *know* it. I protested because I *loved* you."

"You didn't love anybody but yourself."

I could see these six words hit Nell just as clearly as if he had thrown six rocks at her in quick succession.

"That's not true," Nell said, her voice breaking. "You want it to all be that simple. But war is *not* that simple, Stanton. Life is not that simple. It's all way more complicated than that."

"You're telling *me* about war? You went off and now you think you're better than me, smarter than me," Daddy said. Still he had not looked at her. He put his eyes on my mother and let out a single laugh, as if to emphasize the ridiculous nature of his own sentence. "Than all of us. You think you're so smart, so high and mighty with your big ideas and your—"

"That's a black lie!" Nell yelled, standing on the last word. She stood there like a half-prepared boxer. Her legs were firmly planted, her arms hanging down at her sides. "You're the one who went off on a big adventure. You make me sick, saying you were fighting for your country. You went there looking for a big time, and then you found out that it was a war. It wasn't an adventure; it was *real*. And now you're pissed off at the rest of the world because you think nobody warned you. But we by God all warned you!"

Daddy bolted up, grabbed the Gibson by the neck, swung it through the air in one perfect-circle arc. The guitar crashed into the wooden chair where he had just been sitting, a clanging of strings and wood.

"Mommy's guitar!" Nell screamed.

The body of the guitar was hanging onto the neck only by the bronze strings. Daddy let his fingers uncurl from the neck and tossed the Gibson aside. He was wild-eyed, breathing hard. He looked down at the guitar as if he had just realized there was a dead body lying at his feet.

He stepped out of the circle of chairs, where only a few minutes before I had been thinking of what a blessed night we were having. I looked at the guitar lying on the grass, and Nell, hunched over in her chair, pulled up inside herself the way she sometimes did. There was my mother at Daddy's heels as he stormed into the house by way of the screen porch, Josie down on her knees in the yard, holding the neck of the guitar in one hand and clutching the body with the other, looking as if she thought she might be able to put them back together. "He was supposed to give it to me someday," she said, as if dumbfounded. Charles Asher, suddenly small and stupid, peered down at her.

I couldn't help it: I hated Daddy.

Nell wasn't one to cry, but I believe she shed a tear or two before she could take charge of herself. She wiped her face with the backs of her hands and squatted down next to Josie, her hand flat on her back. Josie flinched away from her, and a shocked look spread itself out over Nell's face.

"I'm sorry," Nell said. "I didn't mean to ruin such a nice night."

Josie stood up, slow and careful, as if moving too quickly would set off somebody else. When she had completely stood, she said, "It's not your fault. It's nobody's fault." She wasn't very convincing, and I knew why. Like me, she was always torn between her loyalty to Daddy and what felt like the truth. But we all knew it was the war's fault. Nobody else's.

Nell kept her eyes on the guitar. She let out a strange

little moan, maybe picturing my grandmother playing the guitar way back in time. Nell tucked the body of the Gibson into the grip of her arm and took hold of the guitar's neck with one hand. None of us spoke as she walked across the yard, carrying her mother's guitar with her into the house where she would hide its corpse away in her room.

FOURTEEN

We were all in bed, but none of us was asleep when the headlights slid through my bedroom window. I could hear Josie's and Nell's muffled talking over in their room beside me. There was no noise from my parents' room, but I knew they were still up. We were never made to go to bed early in the summertime, as my mother believed we ought to wring every moment of freedom out of our days. But none of us could bear to look at one another after Daddy broke the guitar, so we went to bed. We didn't know why we were all ashamed, but we were.

I was lying propped up against several pillows, writing in my notebook about what I thought of Anne Frank. After finishing a big chunk of diary, I had just written *I believe that Anne Frank is becoming one of my heroes* when the car pulled in next door. I snapped off my lamp and scrambled up onto my bed so I could look out my open window undetected. As soon as I put my face against the screen, the crickets sounded louder, but I could hear car doors slamming and then footsteps up the side of Edie's house as people made their way to her back door. All was darkness out there in the space separating our houses, but I knew someone was moving about, even though they weren't saying a word. When the light popped on in the kitchen windows, I knew that Edie was finally back. I couldn't imagine where they'd been so late.

I tugged on my cutoffs that I had let crumple to the floor beside my bed and slipped out of my room, easing the door open and shut, tiptoeing down the hall. I scurried past my parents' room and slid out the back door like a breath, scampering across the backyard with the grass warm beneath my bare feet. The moon that had lit the yard earlier was now high and smudged silver behind a haze that I knew was heat.

Just as I reached her window, Edie's bedroom light came on. If I put my eye right up to the edge of the shade, I could see in. The window screen was gritty with dirt. There she was, pausing for a moment with her hand still on the light switch, looking at her room as if she had never seen it before. She moved like an old woman over to her dresser, where she pulled off her watch and laid it down, ran her fingertips along the top of a little Holly Hobbie music box she'd had for ages. I thought she might pick up the box and wind the music, but she didn't.

I rapped on the window with two knuckles, two sudden *tap-tap*s, but she wasn't startled at all. When she appeared at the window, her face was flat and void of any kind of emotion or hint to give me about where she'd been or what she'd been doing all day. She stared at me for a second too long, and I thought she might just stand there without seeing me, but finally she pointed toward the back door and left her room.

She eased out onto the porch as masterfully as I had onto my own. "Let's sit by the willow tree," she said without any sort of hello. She sounded worn out more than tired.

We moved in silence to the base of the willow and were covered up by its scent: green and cool and musky. She put her head back against the trunk and lay her hand palm up on a patch of moss growing over a big root.

"Where you been all day long?"

"We took Mom to the airport," she said.

"Where did she go?"

"Atlanta," she said, her eyes on the night sky. "Her sister

lives there." Edie laughed a little. "She's so psychotic. She thinks she can go down there and become an actress. She really believes that."

"She's moving there?"

Edie nodded, and only then did she look away. She had found a small twig and pressed her thumbs together to spin it between them. She studied this for a long, quiet moment when there was nothing but the night sounds pressing in on us from all sides.

"But who ever heard of going to Atlanta to be an actress? I can see New York or Hollywood. But Atlanta? No. She's crazy, man. And she made a big production out of leaving. Got down on her knees there in the airport and said how much she loved me and how I should always remember that. And she said, 'You've always been my sweet little bird.'" Here Edie paused a long minute, and again there was nothing but the night sounds between us. "She cried and went on and I thought how she really *was* a good actress. And so then she just walked away and we watched her get on the plane and we left and drove back and Daddy never said a word the whole way."

"What makes you think she was acting?"

"Because. If she really loved me, she wouldn't have left me like that, Eli. Real mothers don't just up and leave you. She don't love anybody but herself."

"Don't say that."

"Why not?" Her eyes were hard and dark. "It's the damn truth. I hate her. I hope her plane crashes and she dies."

"Don't say that."

"Stop saying that!" she yelled, then her chin darted around to the back door to make sure her father hadn't heard. She laid the twig down where she had found it. "Just stop talking, period."

I put my hands on the ground behind me, acting as if I was about to get up. "I'll go, then."

Her hand zoomed out and grabbed hold of my wrist, lingered there. I looked down at her curled fingers, then back up at her.

"Just sit here with me," she said, "and the willow tree. Until we get sleepy."

I scooted around so that my back was against the trunk, too. The tendrils of the willow boxed us in, made us feel as if we were in a house made of leaves. It was like being under the snowball bush, except there was wide-open space. And here and there the longing trails of leaves parted so we could see out.

"Look, the moon's coming out of the clouds," she said, and pointed. And at the top of the sky the haze of heat was breaking up so that the moon slid out, white as bones. That was the first time that I realized Edie was my family, too. Just as much as Nell or Josie or my parents or anyone. She was my blood, and I would have died or killed for her.

PART TWO

The Fourth of July

Americans want to be told the truth,
even when it is unpleasant. We have always
responded well to a challenge.

—Jimmy Carter, 1976

Although the fireworks weren't supposed to start until dark, we were to leave in the afternoon, when the sky was still white with July sun. I helped Daddy and Charles Asher carry all the folding chairs from the screen porch out to the truck while the women finished getting ready. Daddy and Charles Asher carried two of the little wooden seats at a time, practically dangling the chairs from their fingertips while I struggled with just one.

When I came around to the back of Daddy's truck, both arms wrapped around the chair, Charles Asher reached down from where he stood on the tailgate and took it from me. "Boy, you're strong, Eli," he said, smiling. He slid the chair into the pickup as if it weighed no more than a sheet of paper and hopped down onto the ground, flicking the bill of my Uncle Sam hat. As we walked back up to the house, he put one hand on my back, right between my shoulder blades. "Thanks for helping us, little man," he said.

I hoped that Josie would start being nicer to Charles Asher, that she might even marry him and then he'd be my brother-in-law and we'd have lots of days of doing things such as loading chairs together.

Daddy and Charles Asher made their place on the screen porch while, back in the kitchen, Josie and my mother and Nell packed us a cooler and stuffed a picnic basket full of sandwiches, chips, and Reese's cups. There would be all kinds of concession stands set up on the square, but my mother saw no sense in paying good money for things we could bring from home.

The door between the kitchen and the screen porch had been propped open, so I stood against the jamb, where I could listen to either conversation by simply focusing my attention on either the men or the women.

I still find it amazing, how easily and completely a child could disappear back then. None of them even realized I was there.

Daddy and Charles Asher were talking about Mustangs.

Their conversation always made its way back to cars some-how. Charles Asher sat differently around Daddy: hunched over in his seat, his hands clasped in front of him while his elbows rested on his knees. He looked like a grown man when he was in Daddy's presence, because he was always careful to make his posture seem this way. Daddy leaned back in his chair the way he always did, looking like the king of this porch, and asked Charles Asher how his oil was doing and then they started talking about the miracles of a 380 engine block and all the other things that people who worship Mustangs bring up.

In the kitchen, Josie was spreading peanut butter onto slices of Bunny bread while Nell put circles of mustard on the baloney sandwiches. Mom filled the red metal cooler full of bottles of Pepsi, 7UP, and Dr Pepper.

"I read in the paper that the county spent ten thousand dollars on fireworks this year," Nell said.

"That's ridiculous," Josie said.

"It *is* ridiculous," Nell said, ripping a piece of wax paper with great force to emphasize the *is*. "There's many a per-son who could have used that money to buy food or clothes. There's people around here who don't even have a box fan, and the county's blowing that kind of money on fire-works."

"So we should be the only county in the entire nation that doesn't have a nice fireworks show?" Mom said.

"No," Nell said. "I'm looking forward to seeing the fireworks. But my God, Loretta, don't you think that's a bit *much*?"

"Well, I know what you're saying," she said, and latched the cooler lid. "But, no, not this year. This year it ought to be done up right. It's the bicentennial, for God's sake."

"Yes," Josie said in a breathless, movie-star voice as she clumped jam onto the bread. "Let's spend thousands to celebrate two hundred years of stealing from the Indians, the Mexicans, the—well, everybody. Let's shoot fireworks off and not even remember all the slaves and the four little girls who died in the Birmingham church and—"

"Stop it," Mom said, firm and final. "Don't talk like this tonight, Josie. Please. It's Independence Day."

"It's true, though," Josie said. She kept her eyes on her sandwich. "I just don't understand why all that's being skimmed over, why all that stuff is being forgotten in this big celebration. And if we're being so patriotic, then why not be true patriots and question all of this—"

"I don't give a damn if it's true or not." My mother never cussed, so I knew she was using this word for special emphasis. It worked; Josie immediately looked up at her, frozen, but with a look of contempt on her face. "I don't want to hear it. We're going to have a good time tonight, whether you want to or not."

Josie gave a brief look to Nell, who nodded and widened

her eyes in a way that suggested Josie should follow our mother's advice and not push it any further.

On the porch, Daddy was saying that the best Mustang ever was the 1964½ two-plus-two. "That swayback," Daddy said. "Man, it was sharp." Daddy talked to Charles Asher the way he did to other men. I supposed he would talk to me in such a way someday, but I couldn't imagine that happening anytime soon.

And then Edie was coming up the steps and opening the screen door to the porch. She looked small, defeated.

"Hey there, half-pint," Daddy said.

Daddy had called her by Pa's nickname for Laura on *Little House on the Prairie,* her favorite show. Edie's face noted this term of endearment, and a look of joy and sadness flitted across her eyes.

"Hey," she said to my father, although she looked at me at first, then back to my father. "Can I ride to the fireworks with you all? Daddy's decided to just watch everything on television tonight."

"Sure you can," Daddy said. "You're welcome to go anywhere with us. You know that."

"I brought these for us," she said to me, and lifted her hand. Only then did I realize that Edie was clutching four or five long boxes of sparklers. Edie handed me a couple of the boxes, and I looked down at the labels. Across the box was written HAPPY BIRTHDAY AMERICA SPARKLERS and, in smaller letters, *Show your patriotism in brilliant flashing lights!*

"You wearing that hat?" Edie asked.

"Yeah, it's cool."

"I guess," she said, curving her words to let me know she didn't think so.

"You all ready, then?" my mother said, suddenly right behind me as I stood in the door.

"We were born ready," Daddy said.

SIXTEEN

My parents rode up front, but Nell had climbed in the back of the truck with Edie and me. Nell sat on the floorboard (Edie and I were on the little humps over the wheels) and stretched her legs out in front of her. She wore a long paisley skirt that flapped up and down in the wind and had brought along a quart jar of sweet tea with the lid tightly fastened. The ice in the jar clinked against the glass and made a bit of music. When we came to a stop sign, she lit a cigarette with her Zippo, which clicked open and shut with a loud, pleasing pop. She lay her head back against the side of the truck bed and closed her eyes, the wind stirring her hair into a wild, red mess. She didn't care. She couldn't very well sit up front because she and Daddy still hadn't spoken since the guitar episode. Supper was often an awkward affair of silverware noise.

I had entrusted my Uncle Sam hat to my mother so it wouldn't blow off my head, but to my disappointment she had laid it on the seat instead of putting it on.

Charles Asher and Josie followed close behind in his shining Mustang. At the next stop sign we could hear the music from Charles Asher's car floating up to us — "Bohemian Rhapsody."

There were people out in their front yards all along the road, lighting fireworks. The daylight was still too bright to see things like Roman candles, but kids were letting off bottle rockets just for the little bang and the trail of blue smoke that arched up into the sky. As we drove by one house a grown man without a shirt lit a pack of firecrackers and threw them out onto the yard, where a group of children scattered like bugs in the shadow of a lifted rock, laughing and squealing. Most everyone waved to us, and Edie and I did, too. Nell lifted her chin in greeting, the way my father did.

The smell of burning charcoal had overtaken the air. This was a pleasing smell that made me hungry. At every other house we passed, there was a man standing at a grill or a woman carrying a platter of chicken down to picnic tables set up on the yards. Children everywhere, running and playing. Free.

I had never seen so many flags in my life. Everybody had one up. They were hanging from porch eaves and poles and clotheslines. They were draped across the backs of porch gliders, fastened somehow to windows, clothespinned to tree limbs. We drove past a barn that had been painted to look like an enormous, stiff flag. "Good God," Nell said to this. Daddy blew his horn to the barn, and Charles Asher did, too.

Once we neared town, Daddy slowed, since traffic was backed up. I stood, leaning on top of the truck's cab, and there was a line of cars that went on as far as I could see. Beyond that were the big steeple at the college, the steeples of the two large churches in town, and the courthouse tower, which was decked out in red, white, and blue bunting. People bobbed down the sidewalk like a sea of bodies, carrying small flags and coolers and chairs.

"I didn't think there were this many people in the entire county," Edie said.

Nell took a long drink of her tea, draining the contents of the jar, and then screwed the lid back on and wiped her mouth with the whole length of her lower arm. "I think I'll walk the rest of the way into town," she said. "Too hot to set in the back of this old truck." On her last word, she threw her legs over the side of the truck and joined the people who were headed toward the courthouse square. As she sashayed off, she hollered to my mother that she'd meet us all up there. I watched her for a long time, as she did not become a part of the crowd, really. Her red hair caught the sunlight and her strong walk set her apart from the others. The crowd parted for her determined march.

I positioned myself on the edge of the truck bed and leaned down into Daddy's window and begged to walk on in, too. He was looking straight ahead, his wrist leaning on the steering wheel and the square muscle in his jaw clenching. He looked over to my mother, and she leaned forward. "You meet us in front of the courthouse in thirty minutes," Mom said. "I want us to all watch the parade together."

Edie and I scrambled out of the back of the truck, waving to Charles Asher and Josie, and then we were part of the thick line of people, too. Here was great chaos, and I liked it. A cop stood in the middle of the street, directing the cars toward a detour to make way for the parade, so eventually we walked in the middle of the street, occasionally running, sometimes skipping. Edie and I fell into a rhythm with this, and it seemed that we could both anticipate the other's next move. All along the street, the houses were close to the sidewalks, with short little yards where people sat out on their porches, considering the passing crowd without any expression on their faces. I couldn't understand how everybody stood living so close to one another like they did in town. It would have driven my mother crazy.

The courthouse square teemed with a thousand people, all darting this way and that like crazed birds. There were stands selling cotton candy and popcorn, candied apples and peanut-butter fudge. A big woman with huge glasses that magnified her eyes concentrated on squeezing lemons for homemade lemonade. A trailer with open sides held a group of army recruiters who hollered at all the teenage boys and told them how much money they could make by joining the service.

Everything was decorated in red, white, and blue, which made me realize that I had left my Uncle Sam hat back in the truck. I grieved over this a few minutes, but there was too much to take in, so I forgot it before long.

The courthouse sat in the middle of the square like a red box cake, its bricks baking in the July heat. The grass around it was unnaturally green, since it was watered every day. Every window was filled with the faces of people who had ventured in for a good view of the parade. All of them waved lazy fans and pushed against one another to feel the barely moving air that made its way to the windows. The radio station was set up near the courthouse steps, and they were playing music way too loud. A girl in a halter top and cutoffs flitted around in front of the big speakers, offering handheld fans to everyone. Most of the girls and women looked at the girl with a sneer and plucked the fan away from her, taking in the whole length of her outfit while the boys tried to strike up conversations with her, which she ignored. She simply called out, "Free fans. Courtesy of WYMR," in a bored repetition while she gave them out. Edie and I were seized by the opportunity to get something free, so we pushed against the crowd until the half-naked girl had given us one apiece. The fans were square with little wooden handles stapled to a thick sheet of paper. On one side there were pictures of all thirty-eight presidents, right up to Gerald Ford. On the other side were the words to the Pledge of Allegiance, the national anthem, and "America the Beautiful."

I started fanning with mine right away, but Edie paused long enough to study hers. "It always seems like Abraham Lincoln is looking you right in the eye," she said. "You ever noticed that?"

"Yeah, it's creepy."

"My mother had a terrible crush on John F. Kennedy," she said, not taking her eyes off the fan. I was busy looking around at everybody.

"That *is* creepy."

"She's so messed up," Edie said. "What's creepy is that she had a crush on him even after he was dead. Her and Daddy got into a big fight about it one time."

It seemed to me that Edie's parents had had a fight about everything at some point, so this held little interest. "Let's go down to the river," I said, and before she could reply, I zigzagged across the courthouse lawn and crossed the street, then ran down the steep bank that led to the river. The shore was crowded with willows that gave a deep blue shade. Cicadas clicked in the branches of the trees, so loud they overtook the din of a thousand voices that drifted down from the street. I liked our riverbank at home much better, as this one didn't seem real. The city workers maintained the grass along the river and had planted little clumps of impatiens around some of the trees. It didn't seem right for something like a riverbank to be kept up; wild things should be free to remain wild. Lots of families had spread out quilts down here and were sitting on them, eating funnel cakes and fried chicken they had bought from the vendors along Main Street. Children were running everywhere, with sparklers sending glints of yellowish silver out behind them or playing catch and freeze-tag. I saw Paul and Matt, so I turned to go, almost running face-first into Edie, but then the boys hollered my name and I knew I'd have to speak to them.

They sauntered over to us, and I caught a glimpse of what they'd be like by the time we reached high school — blond, golden-tanned boys like that one who had said Charles Asher's daddy was a dopehead because he was in the war. I hadn't realized until that moment that I already hated them, even if I didn't want to. I had once truly thought they were my friends. Now I couldn't even imagine wanting to talk to them.

"Well, look, Eli's hanging out with his girlfriend again," Matt said, soliding his hands on his hips. He hooked his thumbs in his belt loops.

"Go eat another turd, Matt," Edie said, and brought up her fan to swipe a breeze against her face.

"And look," Paul said, glancing down to my right hand, which I was trying to put behind my back. He capped his hand over his heart in mock joy. "They've got matching fans. That's really sweet."

"Shut up, ass-face," Edie said.

The boys cracked up at this. They laughed and elbowed each other. "Well, I can see who wears the pants in this marriage," Matt said. "She doesn't let Eli say anything."

"Shut up, man," I said, at last able to make my mouth move. "You think you're cool, but you're not."

"Is that the best insult you can come up with?" Matt said, and drew his fingertips up into his armpits with a hearty laugh. "That's pathetic. You'd think a boy whose mother has the best boobs in the entire world would be cooler than that."

"Don't talk about Loretta that way," Edie said, taking a step forward. "I'll mash your mouth."

"I'm shaking in my shoes," Matt said. "Trembling."

I wanted to hit Matt, but instead I turned on Edie. "I can take up for myself," I said. "So shut up."

When Edie realized I was talking to her, her face changed, flattened. I believe she might have grown up in that moment. Even her posture changed. She looked like a balloon that was beginning to deflate, but then she puffed up again, filled with the defiance and strength that would carry her through the rest of her life. "Do it, then, instead of being a damn coward," she spat. "Don't let them talk about your mother that way."

"Well, she's my mom, not yours." I could feel Paul and Matt watching us. So I added: "Yours left." As soon as I said this, I knew what I had done. I could feel the betrayal crackling in the air, like the ice of an entire river was breaking all at once. I knew what a horrible thing I had just said, but instead of backtracking, I kept going. I made it worse. "So stay out of my business. I could stand up for myself if you'd stop following me everywhere." I was breathing hard, my face heating up, my fists clenched. She was right: I was a coward and I knew it, so I took it out on the best friend I ever had.

Her eyes touched mine for a time. I could feel the boys behind me, waiting to see what would happen. All the sounds of the crowd and the river and everything had fallen away.

"You're no better than them," Edie said at last. She turned and stomped away. The worst part is that I let her. I watched her for a moment, wanting to call out to her or run and catch up with her, but I didn't. I turned back to the boys.

"It's about time you got rid of her," Matt said. Maybe he thought I had chosen him over her, that I was back to the nine-year-old he had known last summer who never thought about anything except playing Hot Wheels and swimming. But now I liked to read and I could hear the trees when they spoke and I was different from them. I was weird and glad of it. Nowadays I actually thought about things, which is that hardest thing to begin doing. The strangest thing was that I liked being different. But it had taken me betraying Edie to know that, so the realization wasn't worth the price.

And maybe for some demented split second I had wanted those boys' approval, had wanted them to ask me to play with them again. But now I hated them more than ever.

"No," I said. "I wouldn't play with you two if you were the last buttholes on earth."

"What'd you call me?" Matt said. Without even glancing that way, just by the curl of his voice, I could tell he was clenching his fists.

So before he had a chance to do it first, I let my fan flutter to the ground and brought my right hand up and smashed my knuckles against his mouth. His buck teeth split the skin on my hand, and blood popped out in three singular bubbles. When he gained his senses, he saw my hand, thought the blood was coming from his lip, and ran away crying to tell his mother. I stood there, looking Paul in the eye, waiting to see if I'd have to hit him, too. But he simply blinked at me a couple of times and took two steps back, then ran along behind Matt, calling for him to wait.

I looked down at my hand and wondered what I'd tell my father. The one thing he had always taught me was to try to avoid violence of any kind. But sometimes it is unavoidable. Like that moment in the jungle when he had to look right in that man's eyes and kill him. Because if he hadn't, my father would have been the dead one. Like this moment, when I had to let these boys know that I was done with their games, that I chose myself over them. But no, I knew that I could have just walked away. It would have been the harder thing to do, but I could have done it.

I trudged down to the river and put my hand in the water, watching it as if from very far away, as if I had floated above myself and was looking down, judging this little boy on the bank who was washing blood from his knuckles. The water was warm and immediately comforting to the smarts of pain that ran all the way to the tips of my fingers. I had the sudden urge to taste the river. I brought my hand around to cup up some of the water, but when I put it to my mouth, all I could taste was blood.

SEVENTEEN

My family was situated on the sidewalk near the courthouse, laughing and talking as they sat in the wooden chairs they had carried down after they parked. I stood in the milling crowd and studied them before they had a chance to see me.

Nell was nowhere to be found, but Josie had already bought a bag of cotton candy and her lips were purple from eating it. Charles Asher had his arm stretched out across her shoulders, a crooked little smile playing out on his face.

My parents were similarly hugged up, too, but my mother was paying more attention to Edie than to my father, who ran his thumb up and down my mother's arm as he looked around, taking in all the people who had ventured out for the parade and fireworks. Edie was sitting on the curb, leaning back against my mother's legs. Mom was bent over and talking to her, but Edie only sat there with her arms hugging herself, nodding. Her face was still square, and I knew that Edie hadn't told what happened and was being questioned about where I was. My mother could tell something was wrong with Edie; I knew because she put her hand out and smoothed it over Edie's head, five or six long strokes that caused Edie to close her eyes. No one could see her face but me. I couldn't remember the last time my mother had touched me in such a way.

I made my way over to them.

My mother looked up with her eyebrows fretted. "You were supposed to be here ten minutes ago," she said. "Don't ever go off by yourself like that again. I told you and Edie to stay together."

I apologized and she smiled halfheartedly, letting her anger go so as not to ruin the day.

"Did you bring my Uncle Sam hat?"

"No, I'm sorry, I forgot it in the truck," Mom said.

I sat down on the curb next to Edie, and the concrete sidewalk scorched the backs of my legs. I slid my hands under my thighs and leaned into Edie, but she wouldn't look at me. I wanted to apologize, but instead I just sat very close to her. I thought when our arms touched, my skin would shoot out little messages of penance, but it didn't work. She scooted away. She could read my mind, anyway; she'd feel my grief. And before I could say anything else, the parade started.

At first there were just a bunch of police cars, all of them with their lights flashing blue. The cops wore big sunglasses and looked straight ahead, as if the interest of safety and protection depended on them not looking anyone in the eye. Then came the high-school marching band. The horn players stomped by first, holding their trumpets and saxophones and flutes out stiffly in front of them while they walked in beat to the tapping of the drumline. Then, right on cue, all the horns came up to their lips and they started playing "You're a Grand Old Flag" while they bobbed their clarinets and cornets back and forth in front of them, and a jagged line of girls behind the band thrust their flags into the air and waved them with such force I could hear them flapping even over the music. Lots of people started bouncing around to the music, and everyone was happy and caught up in the parade, except for me and Edie. My mother was clapping her hands to the song, and Charles Asher let out a wolf whistle.

All the floats were done up in some patriotic way. The First National Bank of Refuge's float was a giant Liberty

Bell made of dyed Kleenex, with bank tellers dressed as Betsy Ross walking alongside, throwing suckers to the crowd. A scattering of Dum Dums skidded to the toes of my and Edie's shoes, but neither of us had even bent forward to get the candy before the little kids on either side of us burst in and snatched them up. The college's entry was a man dressed as Paul Revere, sitting on the back of a beautiful chestnut horse that stomped diagonally down the street and looked around wild-eyed every time the tuba sounded. The man, who was too fat and soft-faced to play Revere, shouted, "The British are coming! The British are coming!" in a very unconvincing way while he waved to the crowd. Everyone laughed as he passed. The chamber of commerce sponsored a float that was made to look like Washington's crossing of the Delaware; the JC Penney employees were the wounded and nurses of a Revolutionary War hospital. There were scenes of the Declaration of Independence being signed, and the high-school debate team was dressed in period garb, sitting on the float in front of the principal, who was dressed like Lincoln and delivered only the first line of the Gettysburg Address over and over while he held on to one lapel. Josie burst out laughing at this one. There was a Boy Scout troop and the high-school ROTC, looking especially sinister and stoic. A string of fire trucks held the county's assorted cheerleaders on its back. They all smiled down with Vaselined teeth, and suddenly the captain started clapping as if her life depended on it and began a cheer: "Firecracker, firecracker, boom boom boom. Refuge Redbirds go zoom zoom zoom."

But then one of the fire trucks let out a deafening wail from its siren, and at first I only noticed that several people were laughing and covering their ears, looking around at each other. A baby wailed. I didn't yet realize that behind me, my father had been so startled by the loud noise that he had jumped from his chair, sending it to fall back against the knees of people who stood too close at his back. He stood, hands suddenly out in front of him, his eyes wide, his head darting around like a frightened bird's. My mother rose and put her hands on his arm carefully, the way some of the men walking alongside the horse had tried to steady it when the tuba boomed too loud.

I read her lips over the noise of a group of cloggers who were making their tap-heeled way up the street. "It's all right," she said. "Only a fire truck." I could see him relaxing—it was a visible thing that started by a slump in his shoulders and continued down his arms and chest—and finally, he sat back down. Some teenage girls standing behind him snickered into their hands.

About this time, Nell came floating up the sidewalk, smoking a cigarette with one hand and eating a caramel apple with the other. Charles Asher took his arm off the chair he had been saving her, and she plopped down, digging the toe of her sandal into my leg to say hello. I wished

I had my composition book so I could write down every-thing I wanted to remember. Lately I had been trying to use my mind to do this better, for just such occasions when I didn't have my notebook handy.

Half the parade was made up of beauty-pageant queens and runners-up. They all sat atop the backseats of freshly waxed cars. Charles Asher commented on each vehicle as being sharp, souped up, too flashy. When my father had himself back together, he joined in, identifying the make and model of every car. Miss Refuge was in a powder-blue 1968 Corvette. I thought she was ugly, with too much green eye shadow and lips that looked huge by way of glopped-on lipstick. Her smile was fake, as was her wave. She held all her fingers together closely and did no more than tip her hand back and forth through the air. Then there was the high-school homecoming queen from last year, the county queen, all the way up to the state queen, who was even faker-looking than the rest of them. She wore a huge tiara that caught the sunlight and a dark blue dress that matched the Cadillac in which she was riding.

Josie made fun of all the beauty queens as they passed. "Horse teeth," she'd say to no one in particular. Or "She stuffed her bra — it's so obvious." Or "Is it a requirement to have no soul to be Miss Refuge?"

Then all down the sidewalk we could see anyone who was seated rising. Their standing up was accompanied by a wave of rustling that made its way to our ears. Then the clapping started, and we could see who everyone was honoring: the veterans of World War I, who were all being wheeled along in wheelchairs or hobbling along behind walkers. Then the World War II veterans, who got a louder applause and seemed much cockier in their medals and pressed uniforms. And then the Korean War veterans, who didn't get as much feedback but still seemed to walk along very proudly, waving with their arms high in the air or saluting people in the crowd. But there were no veterans of the Vietnam War in the parade. I started to comment on this to my father, but when I turned to him, I could see his own recognition of this in his eyes and I knew that it was something I shouldn't mention. My mother looked as if she were trying to overlook the great disservice that had just been done to my father. Her face showed that she had realized, too, but she continued to clap without actually looking at anything at all. Before long she noticed me staring at the two of them and looked down, then nodded her chin back toward the street to redirect my attention back to the parade.

The ladies' auxiliary had baked a flag cake about the size of a car hood and were wheeling it down the street on a specially made wagon that had several handles running down its side so the old women could push it. They were all dressed in similar flower-patterned dresses, and a few of them had walked so far and hard that their slips had worked down to peek out from under the hems. They were gray-haired and small-eyed and looked especially pleased to be taking part in the parade.

"Hey, I've got a great idea!" Nell said in the cheery voice she used to signal sarcasm. "Children are dying of hunger, so let's bake a gigantic cake and let it melt as we wheel it down the street. It'll be great!"

Josie let out a peal of her good laughter.

"Shut up, Nell," my father said without taking his eyes from the parade. This was the first time he'd spoken to her since he'd destroyed the guitar.

"It's so easy to bake a cake, though," Nell said, with some amount of apology in her voice. "To hold a flag."

My father still didn't look at Nell. I was turned almost completely around now, my eyes on my family instead of the festivities. "Some of those women lost sons in the war," he said, and Nell looked embarrassed, but didn't reply, so he added, "You think *that* was easy? What's easy is to judge too quick, to jump to conclusions."

Nell looked more taken aback than I had ever seen her before. She didn't reply to him. Instead, she made a curling motion with her finger, which was a signal to me that I should turn around and watch the parade instead of her face.

The parade went on for ages, it seemed. More beauty queens, more cop cars, more floats, more Shriners marching past in their fezzes and brown suits. Somehow I found it all very sad. I wasn't exactly sure why. Maybe because I didn't have Edie to enjoy it with because she wouldn't speak to me. But it was more than that. Somehow, I believed that we were all celebrating something we didn't completely understand or agree upon. My history teacher, Mr. Worley, had said that America was a very young nation, which puzzled everyone in my class when we put his statement together with the fact that this was the country's two hundredth birthday. Two centuries seemed like an eternity to us. But now I thought I knew what Mr. Worley meant. We were young because we hadn't really figured ourselves out yet.

When it had finally ended, with a line of majorettes twirling batons high in the air as the band played the national anthem at an abnormally fast pace, I leaned over to Edie and whispered, "I'm sorry."

She kept her eyes on the street, watching the baton twirlers passing. Her mouth barely moved when she spoke. "Go to hell," she said.

EIGHTEEN

Soon the gloaming stretched itself out over us and all was bathed in the rosy glow of a slowly dying evening. The heat did not die down. In fact, it somehow became more noticeable. The air was heavy with the metal smell of sparklers and firecrackers, which rattled constantly down by the river, sending my father into little starts that ran up his right arm and trembled up his neck, causing a tremor to run across the large vein in his forehead. He was a nervous wreck with all that noise about him, but he didn't complain. When some kind of small explosive wasn't making its sound known, then people were calling out happily to one another, or an announcement was being made on a loudspeaker, or pumping music played on the big speakers in front of the courthouse. Sometimes he looked embarrassed when he jerked his head around at the sound of a thumping drum or crashing cymbal. Other times he jumped at the yapping of firecrackers and got mad at himself for being so leery.

I watched his reactions with a mix of wonder and amusement. I had never seen my father scared of anything in his life. I had seen him exposed to loud noises plenty of times, but this was different. Beads of sweat stood on his brow. But we all tried to deny what was happening. I believe we knew, even if we didn't want to admit it to ourselves. The war had come back for my father.

This had been happening on and off awhile now, but on that bicentennial evening, it bloomed like a plume of smoke. Maybe it was the celebration itself, the fervent patriotism that everyone was surprised to see once again, as no one had been particularly patriotic since before the war. Or maybe it was the news that obsessed my father: the union of South and North Vietnam had occurred only two days before that Fourth of July, and he made it known that he was greatly bothered that there now existed a country called the Socialist Republic of Vietnam. If the war had played out differently, there would have been democracy instead of communism there, he said. Perhaps the breaking point for him was seeing that his community had not acknowledged the service of Vietnam veterans in their grand parade. That had hit him like a punch to the kidneys.

He tried to cover up all of that this evening, though. The war played out in his eyes, but his face was a complete mask. He smiled and laughed, tousled my hair, bought cotton candy for Edie and a mood ring for Josie at one of the booths set up along Main Street. As my parents walked in front of us, he spread out his big hand on my mother's back, her slender shoulder bumping into the warm space under his arm. They swayed like a movie-star couple, so confident and beautiful. I can still see them that way so clearly, as if their image at that age has been burned into my brain. It is a puzzlement. I am not sure if it is imagined or not, but I recall everyone on the street turning to look at my parents as they moved along the sidewalk. In that summer when it seemed many marriages were crumbling, my parents' union was an illuminated thing, shining for everyone to see. Their love for each other caused a white light to announce them. He kept his hand on the small of her back. She looked up at him, already laughing as she pointed her long finger out toward something she wanted him to see. They were magnificent.

They floated through the crowd, my father nodding to people he knew, my mother occasionally hugging one of her former students. Some of them told her she was still their favorite teacher or that she had changed their lives or that they missed her since graduating. Edie and I shuffled along at their heels, not speaking, a palpable distance simmering between us. Nell swayed behind us, looking up at the sky, the flag-draped courthouse, taking in everything, as she always did. Charles Asher had moved everyone's chairs over to the courtyard after the parade, and he and Josie sat there waiting for us. On the courthouse porch the DJ and the lazy, half-naked girl were handing out numbered pieces of paper that people latched to their clothes with safety pins. The whole time the DJ talked into the microphone with its cord snaking behind him as he walked back and forth. The speakers pumped visibly every time he spoke in his over-blown newscaster voice.

Josie whispered and laughed about most of the dancers who were moving pretty pitifully to "Let Your Love Flow" by the Bellamy Brothers. Only one girl had surrendered to the music like my mother did, and she was the best. She had a tight red braid that struck her below the waist. She closed her eyes and let the music take control of her, her arms swimming through the air, everything about her moving. "She's beautiful," Nell said, and everyone's silence agreed. But besides her, everybody else was pathetic. Still, the song made us all tap our feet. Edie watched with a blank, firm face. She looked completely washed out.

After a couple more songs, the winners were picked and we booed when the prize went to a boy who had only been showing off and not really feeling the music. The redbraid girl sauntered away gracefully and my mother called out to her that she should have won. The girl smiled and said, "Thank you, Mrs. Book," addressing my mother by her teacher name.

Then the DJ screamed into his microphone — causing my father to lift both his feet off the ground in surprise — that it was time to do the Twist, and then he put the needle to the record and the song started and everyone seemed to get up at the same time, rushing to the makeshift dance floor on the porch or on the grassy yard.

The music twined and built, and everyone's joy seeped out over the crowd as if a bucket of paint had been spilled. And then my mother was rising, slipping off her Aigner sandals. She couldn't stand it anymore; she had to dance. She was an expert twister, going up and down, holding one arched leg up in the air as her lone foot twisted, then both feet on the ground, and she twisted heartily at the waist, smiling the whole time, eyes closed, throwing her head back so that her auburn hair trembled about her shoulders.

I didn't realize she was doing anything out of the ordinary until I heard a mountain of a woman in a big flowered dress lean over to her tiny husband and say, "*My* schoolteachers never acted that way." Then I saw how free my mother was, how she was using her whole body to draw out each note of the song. She shook all over, abandoning herself to the song. She didn't care what anyone thought. She knew that people are never comfortable with others having too much freedom, so all she cared about was the music.

My father beamed while he watched her, moving about and clapping in his seat. Josie cupped her hands up to her mouth and hollered out for her. Charles Asher looked ecstatic to be part of a family such as mine, one where the mother would get up and dance on the courthouse yard and not care what anyone thought. Nell threw her head back and laughed, a release of uncontainable joy.

Every once in a while Mom would glance over at us and smile but mostly she concentrated on her dancing. We were all mesmerized by her, by the music, by the peace and freedom and joy that came at last that day.

NINETEEN

Darkness seeped in at the edges of the sky, a great purpling at first, then the sky became the tight, ripe skin of a plum before blackness and starlight took over. We were all so caught up in the booths and people-watching and dancing that night had settled in before anyone really noticed. I did, though. I had been watching the sky for a long while, mostly because I was anxious for the fireworks to begin, but also because I often looked to the sky for some kind of comfort. The way light changed and shifted was a balm to me.

We all gathered on the riverbank to watch the fireworks. They were let off in the football field just across the river. Some of us lay back on quilts; some sat in wooden chairs, others right on the grass. Children ran here and there; their sparklers burned onto our eyes even after they had fizzled out.

Just like in every other little town across America that year, this was the best fireworks display we had ever seen. Huge showers of red and yellow and green and blue and white exploded on the sky, blossoming like giant willow trees. The booms were huge and square-sounding, echoing several times down the hills lining the river. Between explosions, blue smoke hung in the sky.

The whole crowd expressed satisfaction with each burst of fire. An entire chorus of "Ooooh" and "Ahhh" drifted down the riverbank. After a while, though, a sort of reverent silence fell upon us. All the children stopped running about and screaming, and everyone became still. Perhaps we were all understanding that we had been free for two hundred years, or as free as people can possibly be. I like to think that everyone was filled with a brief melancholy, a moment in which we took into account everything we had, and appreciated it all, and felt blessed and lucky to have been born in this country, in this time and place. Or maybe everyone was taking into account all of the wrongs done to others to gain this freedom, the freedom that had been taken from others for our gain. Things like this were too complicated to think about; they caused a rock to sit in my belly, and even though I had only recently discovered the power of constant thought, I tried to turn my mind elsewhere. Years later I would realize that this was one of the world's great problems, that people often allow themselves not to think. They *choose* to not think, and that's how the whole world gets into trouble. My only excuse that day was that I was a child.

Without them knowing, I looked at all the people I cared about the most as they watched the fireworks bloom on the black-blue night sky.

My parents' faces turned pink with the burst of a red shower above us. My mother had a strange little smile on her face. She looked happy that evening; she didn't know everything was about to be shattered. My father's expression was harder to read. He looked like someone listening to a moving song as he watched the fireworks. He blinked very solidly, didn't take his eyes from the sky. There was something square and final about his face. I wondered if he was back in Vietnam in his mind. Was he seeing the explosions in the fields around him, hearing the screams of his best friends, feeling the pierce of shrapnel in the tender meat of his back and left arm? Maybe he could smell the damp ground, the musky trees.

Nell watched in silence, too, her two front teeth perched on her bottom lip, her eyes wet with nostalgia or dread; I couldn't tell which. Every time I looked at her too long, I always remembered the cancer that lived in her, and that same ice-water feeling ran all over me, which made me want to throw up.

Josie caught me studying her, but she just looked at me for a split second, then back up to the sky. Then she whispered to me: "I wonder if anybody else is thinking of the Indians, and the slaves, and the immigrants, and the way soldiers got sent off to die." Her eyes touched mine again. She seemed young again. "Do you think they are?"

"I don't know," I said, very quiet, as if speaking too loudly might break some spell that had befallen us.

"I keep thinking about this thing I learned in history class last year," she said, watching the sky now. Her face went rose-tinted with the blast of a firework. "At Gettysburg, these soldiers got sent into battle and they knew they were gonna die, but they went anyway. Now *that's* being brave," she said. "So what they did is, they wrote these short little letters to whomever they loved. And the best part is that they tied or nailed the letters to the trees."

I could picture this: a woods above the battleground, decorated by hundreds of little papers filled with cramped, old-timey handwriting. "You know who I think about?" she said. "The soldiers who had to go and collect the letters off the trees the next day."

It was a strange thing to be thinking of on such a night, I guess, but somehow it made sense to me. I just nodded, seeing it all in my mind.

Charles Asher had listened while Josie had related this

story in her whispers. There was nothing on his face except puppy love for Josie, always there, along with that hollow look of pining he always carried, since he knew he could never completely have her. Charles Asher already knew something about longing, and his knowledge was aging him too early. Longing will eat you up from the inside out.

Edie looked as sad as I felt. I knew that I had hurt her badly, but I didn't know how to fix it. She and I had waited for this night for so long, and now I had ruined it. I watched her for the longest time out of the corner of my eye, wondering what she was thinking. I wanted to ask her but was afraid she'd cuss me out again. I hoped she wasn't thinking about her mother, way off in Georgia and probably not even giving a second thought to where Edie was tonight. Edie had been doing okay with her mother's leaving before I had put the hot coal of my words into her open, waiting wound. Her eyes were filled with sadness, but not tears.

I looked out over the crowd, the faces being lit by all the different colors of the explosions, and wondered what they were thinking in this big silence that had spread over all of us. So many complicated thoughts and emotions and secrets. For a little while I felt like I was kin to everybody there, all connected by this night, this nation.

After a long while I stopped watching the faces and the fireworks. Instead, I lay back on the grass with my hands behind my head and studied the moon, wondering what this celebration of fire would look like from up there.

TWENTY

Picture my father's turquoise Ford truck chugging down the road once it broke free of the traffic leaving the celebration. Now the road was open and he was driving the truck along the winding road with one hand at the top of the steering wheel, the other as lifeless as a dead bird atop his left thigh. My mother sat next to him, her head on his shoulder as the wind from the open windows came in to peck at her hair. They did not speak.

Nell and Edie and I had climbed into the back of the truck after the fireworks. We had watched everyone loading up—people throwing chairs into trunks and truck beds, piling into cars. We saw an El Camino—we called it a "trar," half truck and half car—that held twelve people. Children were strewn across their mothers' laps in the front seats of Chevettes. Old women sat in folding chairs in the backs of trucks. Carloads of people nearly drunk with sugar bore small flags: the powder of funnel cakes still on their upper lips, the cotton candy moving in their stomachs, the stickiness of caramel apples on their fingers. The smoke from the fireworks drifted over the town like thin gray clouds.

But now we were bumping down the road toward home. Nell leaned her head against the cab of the truck, and Edie and I sat tight against her on either side. She brought her arms out and put them around our shoulders. She smelled like the sandy rocks we gathered from the river, a sharp, clean scent. Edie and I were both exhausted from the celebration, but also from regret, sadness, and stubbornness. Those things will wear you out, will make you feel like a ghost floating through the world. The moon followed us and fell on Nell's noble face. None of us spoke.

And before I knew it, I had been lulled to sleep there with Nell warm against me and the hot night air swirling around us. Looking back, this is when I recall most clearly how it was to be a child. Only children know exhaustion like that, rest like that. Only a child could sleep so well and comfortably in the back of a pickup truck bobbing over a rough country road.

When we got home, my father climbed up into the back of the truck and gathered me into his arms, hopped down, and carried me into the house. I can vaguely remember this. I came awake for a brief moment—long enough to hear the crickets crying out and to see the stars above me and to realize that I was in my father's arms. He had not carried me in what seemed a very long time, and, being satisfied by this, I let my eyes flutter back together and immediately found my deep sleep once again.

The next day Nell explained that she had walked Edie over to her house, talking all the way, and then she and my mother sat on the porch and chatted while they drank clinking glasses of ice water.

Inside, my father laid me atop my bedspread, took off my shoes and jeans, then pulled the sheet up over me. I wonder if he leaned down and kissed my forehead or at least ran his thumb across my brow. I bet he did.

Nell, who felt too awake to go to bed, had spread a quilt out on the backyard to watch the stars but fell asleep immediately, unaware of her own exhaustion. Josie would find her there—and, since she knew how Nell was, didn't disturb her—when she came home at one in the morning, an hour late from curfew, and stumbled into bed.

"Cacophony" had been one of Edie's dictionary finds. That's what the night sounded like, a cacophony of crickets and cicadas, calling out to the dark. Now look at our house, all the windows dark. Nell lying out in the backyard. I had kicked the sheet off me in my sleep and lay there in my T-shirt and underwear, breathing through my mouth, one arm up behind my head.

Down the hall, my mother lay on her back, asleep, her hands folded on her chest in a casket pose. It always troubled me when I saw her sleeping like that because she always looked dead. My father was clad only in his briefs, lying on his side, his big shoulder rising up like a smooth hill. His underwear glowed when moonlight moved around the room and fell on the bed.

We all had the peace of rest, for a time. But it didn't last. By the time Josie got home, it was already over.

I don't know why I woke up. I was sleeping so hard, lost to blackness. But my mother managed to let one stifled scream escape her throat before he pressed his thumbs into the center of her neck.

I sat straight up in bed, completely and instantly awake. I heard my own gasp as I startled. I sat very still, listening. Nothing for a time, then sounds of a quiet struggle. As if her mouth were full of water, I heard my mother say, "Don't." I jumped off the bed and padded down the hallway. Mom had opened all the windows earlier, and the sound of the crickets outside was nearly deafening. I don't know how I had heard her call out over their singing. I walked through one last crooked patch of moonlight, and then I was at the door to my parents' bedroom. They had left it ajar, and inside I could see a flash of movement that didn't seem real. I pushed the door open with the tips of my fingers.

Daddy was straddling my mother's stomach, his knees pressed into the mattress on either side of her. He leaned over, strangling her with such force that both his arms were stretched out firm and straight, pushing her down so that it appeared the mattress was swallowing her up headfirst. I could see the muscles in his back, taut and speckled by tiny beads of cold sweat. I could not see his face, which seems like a blessing to me now. He made no sound except for his heavy breathing, an animal panting after a long run.

My mother brought one hand up, like someone drowning and reaching for the surface. She curled her hand into a claw and raked it down his arm, leaving thin red lines behind. This didn't faze him. In fact, he seemed to be more intent on killing her. She began to kick her feet against the mattress, then brought her legs up and down as if running in place.

I took one step farther into the room, stripes of moonlight falling on me from the edges of the shades in the windows. The shades breathed in a barely present breeze, then settled back against the windows again.

Outside, the night sounds were screaming.

Daddy was strangling her. I could hear a low, dry gagging in the back of her throat. The muscles in his back moved, flexed. The specks of sweat stood still, like clear beads that have spilled out on a brown table.

One final kick from my mother. Her hand raised but then fell back onto the bed. More gagging, like someone trying to cough up rocks.

The crickets and cicadas and katydids sounded louder and louder and louder on all sides of me, as if they had invaded the house and were easing their way toward me in a great, green circle.

Daddy let out a short, halfhearted moan of grief or terror — I don't know which — and then I somehow became unfrozen. I realized that I had been trying to make my mouth work and that it wouldn't. But finally I was able to speak.

"Daddy," I said. A whisper, really.

But I spoke loud enough for him to hear me, because he jerked his head around, and if not for the shadows of the room, I would have seen his dead eyes. Then he rolled off my mother, his arms limp in front of him, and crashed into the nightstand. I saw his head hit the edge of the little table and leave a short gash above his right eye. Blood bubbled up and leaked down his face. The lamp tottered like a top and then fell to the floor, too. The impact caused the dim light-bulb to come on, but the base broke into dozens of pieces. Daddy fell to the floor beside the bed. A piece of shattered lamp glass pierced his lower back, although I didn't know that at the time. He curled in on himself and wrapped his arms about his calves, his knee pulled up to his mouth. I could see his back move with weeping now.

My mother was lying flat on her back on the bed, and she drew in a great gasp of air, as if she were trying to suck in everything the room offered, a drowning woman out of the water. Then she sat up and put both hands to her neck, coughing and hacking from the back of her throat. She had not cried, had perhaps been too scared to cry, but she shuddered the way someone does after a meltdown. She looked up at me, then away, as if she didn't want me to see her. I was frozen again, unable to move. Besides, a thin layer of broken glass lay on the distance between me and the bed. But my mother brought her arm up and curled her fingers in toward her palm, her eyes large on my own in the gray room. I stepped toward her with caution, using the tip of my bare foot to brush glass away before each step. When I got to the bed, Mom pulled me into her arms, folding me up in her own body. She pressed her flat hand against the side of my face, forcing the other side against her wet chest. She was drenched in her own and Daddy's sweat.

"He was asleep," she strained to say, in a voice like rough wood. I knew that she was saying, *Don't worry. He wasn't trying to kill me. It's all right.* I could hear all of that in those three small words. She put her hand to her throat and massaged it, running her forefinger over her windpipe. Even in the dim light I could see the bruises spreading out across her neck, the bruise on her shoulder, the redness of her cheeks, the sweat on her forehead.

He did not rise up and beg our forgiveness or show us his face. He lay there, mostly unmoving. Every once in a while, though, there would be the click of glass that let us know he was uncurling his arm or legs. Sometimes we would hear the quake of his crying. I had never seen or heard my father cry before. I had not thought him capable of such a thing.

Mom settled back against the pillows, worn out, and pulled me down with her into the crook of her arm. "The war," she said. A witch's voice. I thought she was reassuring herself. It took me a long time, years and years, to understand that she was just trying to comfort me. But back then I didn't believe she cared anything about me.

The night creatures, after having reached full hysteria, calmed down. Maybe because morning wasn't too far away. But maybe because they were aware of what had just happened in our house.

Unbelievably, impossibly, after a long time, I drifted back off to sleep as she trembled against me, as Daddy lay in the broken glass on the floor, trying to understand what was happening to him. I guess he spent the rest of the night that way.

When I awoke in the morning, he was already gone to work. I found my mother at the stove, and at first I thought it had all been a nightmare. But then she turned from the stove where she was boiling an egg and her bruised neck was revealed to me. And then I knew that this was my life.

PART THREE

July

I am looking at trees
they may be one of the things I will miss
most from the earth

— W. S. Merwin, "Trees"

TWENTY-ONE

My mother wore the purple bruises on her neck without shame. She didn't situate herself in high-necked blouses or try to cover the marks with makeup, but walked around with the handprints on her neck. The only thing I ever heard her say about the bruises with any amount of worry was that she hoped they'd be gone by the time school started.

"My students would have a field day with these," she said one morning, looking in the mirror and poking at the discolorations, which were becoming green at the edges.

"I can hear the rumors now about how the biology teacher's husband tried to strangle her to death."

Something had changed in my father's eyes. He didn't look at my mother the same way anymore. He barely looked at her at all in those first few days after he'd strangled her in his sleep. Later I would understand that he was ashamed, that he felt guilty of something that was beyond his control. I imagine that at some point he turned to her and put fingers lightly on the bruises that decorated her tender neck, his eyes on hers. Silence splayed out between them like level water. I picture him apologizing to her in a trembling voice, the words caught somewhere halfway up his throat, finally pulling away as if startled, only to saunter away while she called out to him that it was all right. "Come back," she'd call to him.

I'm sure this happened at some point. But it was a long while before he could acknowledge properly what he had done. It is an awful thing to know that you have hurt the person you love most in the world.

I ought to know, because my father and I had both damaged the most important people in our lives that Fourth of July. In many ways, the hurt I inflicted was worse. For one, I had done it intentionally — whether conscious of it or not, I had been trying to impress the boys — and I had also hit Edie with my words when she was at her most tender, shortly after her mother had abandoned her.

My mother didn't have to forgive my father because even when he was choking her, she knew it wasn't his fault. When she placed any blame at all, it was on the war. Stella had happened by the day after and had burst out crying upon seeing the bruises on Mom's neck. "You have to leave him," Stella had said, but Mom just laughed. "It was just the war, Stella," she'd said. "Just that old war." For two weeks after that night, her voice was raspy and hoarse, her windpipe dented by his big thumbs. When her voice came back to normal, it occasionally went out on her, like a deeply scratched record album that causes the needle to jump ahead on the grooves. Entire words of a sentence would be mouthed but have no sound, lost in the cracks of her voice box. When this happened, she'd shake her head and cough up two words of explanation: "The war."

While my father shuddered at her touch, she became even more intent on saving him from his nightmares and flashbacks. My mother thought that most things could be healed by human touch, so she handled him as much as possible. During supper she would often lay her hand atop his, since he always kept his left hand lying on the table next to his plate. He would let this linger a moment, then slide his hand out from under hers, easy and quick, like someone ripping a tablecloth off without disturbing the dishes. She sat very close to him on the truck bench, lay her head on his shoulder when they sat on the porch glider. She was trying to convince him that she didn't hold anything against him. He had tried to kill her in his sleep, but he hadn't been himself; he had been out of his mind. A night terror, she called it. There was nothing for him to be sorry about, she said.

She might have forgiven him, but I hadn't. I thought that I might truly hate him. I wasn't completely sure about that, but I do know that I was afraid of him. I was even jumpier than he was. One day I wrote this in my composition book: *Daddy scares the hell out of me.* I had never written a cuss word before. And still hadn't said one, although Edie had.

Several mornings I crawled beneath the screen porch, knowing that my mother and Nell were bound to talk about all of this at some point. The dirt was unnaturally cold there and populated by all manners of spiders, but I didn't care. Reading *Charlotte's Web* had cured me of any fear like that. I liked to put daddy longlegs on my palm and let them take high steps up my arm, amazed by how I could barely feel them. They must have weighed no more than an eyelash. I only regretted missing the best part of the morning to go riding. Pedaling through the morning mist was like speeding through a cloud, like flying, and I hated to miss that. But after only a couple mornings, my waiting paid off.

Nell was in her usual place, sitting on the glider, smoking and reading *Angle of Repose,* with which she was obsessed.

Only the day before, she and Mom had driven away in Mom's Cougar and had been gone the entire day under mysterious circumstances. Mom had said they went to the Piggly Wiggly, yet they brought back no groceries. So I figured Mom had gone to the doctor with Nell for a checkup on her cancer. I had been so frantic that I had almost spilled the secret to Josie. I didn't know why I didn't tell her, but somehow it felt wrong. She probably already knew, anyway. She and Nell sat up every night whispering and giggling, and it was a constant source of disappointment to me that our bedroom walls were so thick that I couldn't hear their conversations.

Nell was silent and reading when Mom came out from washing the breakfast dishes, and I was in the perfect spot to listen to them.

"Morning," Mom said, and her voice sounded like rocks being scraped together.

"Loretta, you've got to go to the doctor. Listen at you. Your voice box might be shattered or something."

Dust puffed into my eyes when my mother plopped into the chair just over my face. "It's fine," she scratched.

"And Stanton needs to go to the doctor, too. You know he does, now."

Silence. Apparently my mother was giving a firm shake of the head to let Nell know that she didn't agree because Nell spat out her words rat-a-tat-tat after that, afraid she would be cut off before she could say all she wanted. "It's a stress disorder, Loretta. From the war. I heard about it all the time up there in DC. A friend of mine worked at the Veterans Administration." I could almost feel the frustration sizzling on the air between them, could imagine my mother's steely gaze. "Why are you so damn stubborn?" Nell cried out. "What's *wrong* with him going to the doctor?"

"People are always saying how Vietnam vets are crazy. He's not." She coughed these last words out. I pictured her holding her throat as she spoke, kneading out her sentences one by one.

"For God's sake, nobody's saying he's crazy. He needs some help. He's been carrying that war around with him all these years, and nobody is going to help him unless he asks for it and —"

"Nell, I love you just like my sister," Mom said, and cleared her throat long enough to speak clear for a few words. "But you don't have any right to say anything to him about the war. I've forgiven all that stuff that happened back then, but still —"

I could hear the disbelief in Nell's voice. "Are you out of your mind, Loretta? Forgiven me? What was there to forgive? You agreed with me back then. That war wasn't right, and you know it as well as I do."

"Nell —"

"And you know that *I* never did anything but fight to get the soldiers out of there. I never called anybody a baby-killer. Because that happened to him, he groups all the protesters with those dumb-asses who said that to him in Boston. I was *for* the soldiers."

"A lot of people weren't, though, Nell. You know that as well as I do."

"But that wasn't *me,* Loretta."

"There were two sides in all that—the protesters and the soldiers," Mom said. She was still scratchy-voiced, but at least she could say more than a few words in a row. Still, I could hear the frustration in her mouth; she wasn't able to say all she wanted because her voice wouldn't allow it. "You can't be on both sides."

"It's not about sides," Nell countered.

Another daddy longlegs marched across my mouth and was gone before I could move to sweep him away. Above me there was a long silence. I thought for a moment that my aunt and mother might have disappeared into thin air.

Finally, my mother said, in a voice choked full of grief, "I don't know. All I do know is that he went over to fight for his country, then he found himself fighting for his own life. And you think it's all so simple. That's what has always bothered me about it all, how people think it's so simple and it's *not,* Nell."

"I know that," she said, quiet. "That's exactly what I'm saying. I've never thought it was simple."

"That's the problem, that people want it all to be simple," Mom said, as if she wasn't even listening to Nell now. "And then everybody just misunderstands everyone else, and instead of trying to understand each other, we all just go to war in one way or another."

I was aware of Nell moving — the screech of the glider as she did so was the giveaway — and then sounds as if they were hugging. My mother might have been crying; I couldn't really tell. Even so, I pictured Nell comforting her, taking her hands and wiping my mother's face, then cupping Mom's chin between two fingers and forcing her to look up.

"All of the world's biggest problems boil down to misunderstandings, then, don't they?" Nell asked.

My mother let out a jagged, hoarse laugh. Her voice was getting worse, being erased by each word she spoke. "It can't be that easy to explain, can it?"

"Sometimes it is," Nell said, her voice distant.

I could hear bare feet on the floor but nothing else. After a time I realized that my mother — unable to argue properly because of her voice — had walked away and left Nell without another word. I lay very still for a time and then heard the click of Nell's Zippo and a loud, aggravated exhalation of smoke. Then a page of her book was turned with a rough, aggravated hand.

Just as I was about to sneak out from under the porch and go about my bike riding, I heard feet shuffling on the kitchen floor and then my mother's torn-paper voice: "He couldn't help it, when he did this to me. That's all I'm saying." She must have twirled and left the doorway because Nell didn't say a word.

TWENTY-TWO

Edie was much too defiant to be as forgiving as my mother. She didn't speak to me for more than a week, which seemed like ages and ages. I walked around as if wounded in the gut, lost without her. She was the first person I wanted to talk to after Daddy's fit, but I couldn't run to her bedroom window and tap on the frame because I knew she would only part the blinds with two fingers and then let them snap back together. There was no use in trying to get her to talk to me because I knew she wouldn't do it until she was ready.

She might never have forgiven me if she hadn't been forced to seek peace at my house that night.

Nell and I had decided to sleep out on the screen porch, as it was unbearably hot. The little air conditioner in the living room had run so hard and long that it had finally frozen up, so Daddy just snapped it off for good, opened all the windows, and turned on the three box fans we owned. I spent a great deal of my time sitting in front of one fan, saying long, complicated sentences that the fan blades would distort and chop into syllables that didn't exist. I was on the camping cot because Nell opted to sleep on a little pallet she had made on the floor. I had been raised well enough to protest, knowing that my elder should get the cot while I took the floor, but she said sleeping on the wood planks would help her back.

For a long while I sat up in my cot and wrote in my composition book. I had decided to write a short story about the little fox that I believed to live up on the ridge. I had never seen him, really, but I had felt him. I was trying out first lines of the story but wasn't getting much past that because Nell kept interrupting my thoughts. She was still reading her thick book and had to pause occasionally to read me a line or a passage she liked. Some of them I didn't understand, others I did, but to each I just gave a short "Mmm-hmm" so I could get back to my own writing.

We both lay down and were silent, listening to the katy-dids, cicadas, crickets, frogs, and other creatures that we could not name. I liked the cicadas best. They sounded ancient. The moon drifted behind a moving black sky streaked with silver clouds, only giving occasional light to us.

After a time, Nell finally said, "Sometimes I wonder why I ever left this place. Ran off to New York and DC and Atlanta and just all over hell and back. What was I thinking?"

"I want to go live in New York City someday," I said.

"I do love New York. But it's a hard place to live, Eli. Once you get out of college, you ought to go live there for maybe one year, get that out of your system, and then come home."

"I don't think I'll go to college."

"Oh, yes, you will, buddy. Your mother will make sure of that."

"You didn't."

"And I regret it now."

"You didn't come home after a year," I said. I was in a challenging mood and didn't know why.

"And I regret that, too," she said, her voice changing as she rolled over onto her side. I stared at the shadows on the porch ceiling. "Sometimes I do. But I wouldn't change my life."

"Did you get fired from your job in Washington?" I had been dying to ask her this for a long time. She had worked for some kind of civil rights department, editing its magazine. Matt had once told me that he overheard his parents saying that Nell worked for a Communist newspaper, but when I asked her about that, she had said Matt and his folks were idiots.

"No, I quit." I could hear her fumbling around on the floor, then the crack of her Zippo, and for a moment her face blazed up orange as she lit her cigarette. I hadn't realized how close she lay beside my cot. "I wanted to come home awhile."

"You missed us all too bad?" I asked, knowing that she had come home because she was sick. I guess I wanted her to say that she needed us during her time of trouble.

"Well, yeah, of course I did," she said, then for a long moment I was aware of her collecting her thoughts. It is strange how our senses become in the dark. I knew for certain that she was thinking, preparing what she would say next, just as I had been certain that she was still awake while we had lain there listening to the night sounds. "But I missed the trees, too."

"They have trees in Washington, though."

She exhaled smoke loudly. "But there's not a tree in the world like the ones you grow up with. You never forget them, and the trees remember you."

It seemed to me that every time I had a conversation with Nell I had another reason to worship her. I knew that my father felt as if she had betrayed him during the war, and a small part of me held that against her, but her whole being usually kept that pulsing doubt about her at bay. Besides, my loyalties to him grew weaker every summer day. I sat up on one elbow, looking down to the red dot of her cigarette. "If I tell you something, will you keep it secret?"

"You know I will."

"I can hear the trees. If I put my hand up to them, and concentrate? They talk to me."

"What do they say?" She was completely serious, not mocking or making fun of me the way many people might have replied to my confession.

"Well, it's not like words, really. It's more like a feeling, like they're speaking to me. I don't know; it's hard to explain. Seems like they're always saying, over and over, 'I am here.' But at the same time, I never really hear those words, but I know that's what they're saying."

She was silent. There were only the cicadas and crickets, a little breeze that slithered through the valley and set the chimes to ringing out a bit.

"Do you think I'm crazy?" Sometimes I thought I might be.

She sat up and just enough moonlight fell on her that I could see her face, but her eyes were lost to the shadows. "No," she said. "I think you're one of the best people I've ever known in my life, Eli."

"Why do you say that?"

"Because you pay attention. Most people don't."

"You hear them, too, then?" I didn't know why I was whispering.

She put out her cigarette and lay back down. I imagined that she had brought her hands behind her head, staring up at the darkness between us and the ceiling. A short, thinking pause. "Well, yeah, I guess I do. But I never realized it before you said that, before you explained it. That's exactly how it feels, though, to lay your hands on certain trees."

A great crack broke the night in two, causing the insects to momentarily quiet down but not completely stop. Nell and I both shot up in our beds before we realized it had only been the slam of a screen door, so close that it could only be Edie's. And by the time we had collected this information for ourselves, someone was tugging at our own screen door, which I had latched against the outside.

"Eli?" Edie said, her voice full of hurt. "Are you there?"

"It's me," I said, so happy to hear her say my name again. I scrambled across my cot to unlatch the door for her. Nell slipped her hand inside the kitchen door to turn on the porch light, and we were bathed in its yellow glow.

Edie was not one to fall against me, sobbing, but her gathered brow showed that she wanted to. She was too stubborn to cry, but it was clear that something was wrong. It seemed to me that she had completely grown up in the week we had been apart. She knew things that I did not, and her face made this clear.

"What is it?"

"I just don't want to be in that house with him," she said, and looked at the floor, embarrassed.

Nell did not move from her place by the door. "Did he do something to you?"

"No," Edie said, her big eyes touching Nell's. "He's passed out drunk. I just can't stand to be in there with him like that."

Nell came forward and leaned over to put her hands on Edie's shoulders. "Well, I'll just make you a pallet here beside me and everything will be all right. He's just going through a hard time right now."

"He must not care that I'm having a hard time with this, too, then," she said. "He can get drunk, but what am I supposed to do?"

Nell held Edie against her, and Edie brought her hands around Nell's waist with hesitation. She looked at me briefly, ashamed, but then she closed her eyes. "Is Loretta here?" she asked, her voice muffled against the extra-long T-shirt Nell wore as a nightgown.

Nell stepped back and looked down at her, realizing that Edie needed a mother right now but that Nell herself would not do. Nell wasn't insulted by this, though. She understood instantly. "I'll go get her up," she said.

And then it was just me and Edie there on the porch while Nell went to get Mom. There were the crickets and frogs growing louder around us. She looked at the floor and I looked at her.

"Edie, I'm—"

"Don't say anything, okay? Just forget it. I know." She looked completely alone in the world.

I hadn't been about to apologize because I believed that what I had said to her was unforgivable anyway. But I had wanted to say something. I sometimes wonder what words my mouth was going to conjure up in that moment.

My mother came out, looking prettier than I had ever seen her. Her hair was mashed flat in the back and her eyes were sleepy, but she nearly glowed, her skin a deep peach in the porch light. The bruises at her neck shone in the stark light of the yellow bulb. She had put on her summer house-coat and was still snapping the little pearl buttons when she came out the door with Nell close behind.

"Oh, baby," she said, and gathered Edie up in her arms. That's when Edie finally started crying. She hid her face from me within the folds of my mother's silky housecoat, but I could tell by her drawn-up shoulders. Now I had seen the grief of the two strongest people I knew. And somehow, Daddy's and Edie's crying made them seem even stronger to me. It was better to cry than to suck it up and go around conjuring hate in your heart. That's what I had overheard

Nell saying about Daddy. Mom directed Edie toward the house and whispered to her as she went through the door. "You come in here and get in Eli's bed. I'll lie down with you until you get to sleep, okay?" And then they were lost to the shadows of the kitchen and Mom's voice trailed off down the hallway.

Nell sat down on the glider and lit another cigarette. She crossed her legs at the ankle and looked down at her toes. "I swear to God, I just don't understand that girl's daddy," she said. "Is she invisible to him?"

"I'm going to check on her," I said, and hurried into the house before Nell could protest. I moved on into the shadowy kitchen and down the hall on quiet feet. Mom had closed my bedroom door, but a rectangle of yellow showed around its frame from the light within. I put my ear against the cool wood of the door and listened.

"I miss her," Edie said in a low, choked voice. I imagined her sitting up in the bed, her hands to her face.

"The best thing to do is keep on missing her, honey. Until it finally dulls itself out," Mom said. "I never even had a mother. Did you know that?"

Apparently Edie nodded.

"Not that I remember at all, I mean. I grew up in an orphanage. It wasn't until I met Nell that I knew what a family really was. She introduced me to Stanton and her mother, and all at once I had a family of my own."

Edie was silent, perhaps responding only with a look on

her face. There was really no other way for her to reply to all of this information, though. Adults seldom spoke so honestly to children.

"Sometimes you get dealt the wrong hand and you have to find yourself a family, create one for yourself," my mother said, speaking from experience. "So when you feel alone, you can know you have us, for one. All right? We'll always be your family."

Edie must have given a feeble nod.

"The best thing for you to do is to just keep crying, Edie. I hate to tell you that, but that's the only thing that really works. Because one day—just out of nowhere— you'll realize that you're sick of crying over her. And in the meantime, all of us are here if you need us."

Edie started to say something else—what was probably going to be the best part of this whole conversation—when a hand twirled me around. Nell was leaned over and her face was very close to mine. "Eli, don't," she breathed into my face. She grabbed hold of my wrist and pulled me down the hallway.

Once she had shoved me back out onto the dark porch— now spotted with moonlight—she sat down on her pallet and kicked at the covers with her feet, looking up at me with fretted eyebrows. "Sometimes eavesdropping is just not cool, Eli. That was wrong of you, to listen in on Edie like that."

I looked away. I could never remember Nell jumping

on me for anything. "I was just worried about her," I said, which was only half a lie.

Nell was fluffing her pillow. "Maybe you were, but you were also listening when she wouldn't have wanted you to. And that's wrong."

I rolled over and faced the screens instead of Nell. I could feel her disappointment standing in the night air between us. Even if it wasn't a big falling-out, I still couldn't stand the thought of not having her full respect.

After a time I realized that Nell had gone to sleep—her breath caught in the back of her throat, causing little half-hearted moans to escape each time she exhaled—but I lay there a long while, listening to the night sounds, wondering if Edie was doing the same.

TWENTY-THREE

The cry of a morning cicada, high and shrill, like a tiny scream that climbed until it contained a note of pure panic in announcing the day's heat. A moment of blinding light as my eyes came open. And then I saw Edie sitting on the glider, eating from a bowl of Froot Loops while she studied me.

"You sleep like the dead," she said, talking around the cereal.

"What are you doing?"

She nodded toward her house. "Waiting. Loretta went over there to talk to Daddy."

"What about?" I rubbed the sleep from my eyes. It had taken me a minute to remember that something stood between Edie and me now. But she was talking to me in her normal tone, at least. It was as if she had decided to pick up our friendship again. Maybe she appreciated the fact that I had seen her at her lowest and hadn't made fun of her, the way some people might have done. I'm sure that I would have not been big enough to forgive her if she had said the things to me I had said to her.

"I guess she's lining him out. She said he needed help, that he was depressed." She swung her bare feet, one time a piece. "But he's just a drunk."

"He misses your mother," I said.

"Last night, before he passed out, he told me he was going to cut down my willow tree." She let her spoon fall into the bowl with a small clank. I could see the milk in there, turned a sickly pink by the few remaining circles of soggy cereal. "I said if he did I'd leave and never come back. I told him I'd hitchhike to Atlanta. Or kill myself." She turned the bowl up and drank down all the pink milk, then wiped her mouth on her forearm. "I'd never do that, but he doesn't know that."

"He was just talking out of his head." I was trying to think of the right things to say and I didn't know whether I was succeeding or not. Her face did not reveal her feelings. She looked out at the garden, where Stella was hoeing her green beans.

"I'd sure never go to Atlanta. I hope I never see her again."

I sat up, threw the sheet off, and let my bare feet come down hard on the porch floor. "You want to read some more of Daddy's letters?" I said. I had run out of comforting words and didn't know what else to say.

"No," she said, without further explanation. "But we could go swimming, after he leaves and I can get my bathing suit."

I was getting braver. Or maybe stupider. My mother always said there was a fine line between the two.

Braver because I had snuck into my parents' bedroom while Mom was at home. She was out on the porch with Edie and Nell, explaining to Edie that her father was having a hard time accepting her mother leaving and that he was going to try to do better. I watched her from the door a long time, then said I was going to put on my cutoffs. After I did, I skipped into her bedroom, opened the box — a great wash of cedar scent rushing up over me — and grabbed the stack of letters from within. I took them into my room, put aside the ones I had already read, and stuffed the rest into my canvas bag that I sometimes strapped to the back of my bicycle. I was very careful with them, afraid I might bend or harm them in some way, so before putting them into my canvas satchel, I had sealed them in a plastic sandwich bag I had lifted from the pantry.

I hung my satchel on a high hickory limb so that our

splashing wouldn't reach the letters that lay within like a promise. Then I took a high-stepping run and pressed my toes against the sandy rock, pushing my body up into the air before I pulled my legs up, latching my arms around them so I could make a perfect cannonball. I hit the water and plummeted down until my feet touched the bottom of the river. The ground there was so cold that it sent stints into my legs.

It's miraculous, the wild places that exist in hiding. All the secret places of the world that are able to remain cold despite the hum of a blazing summer.

I sat down there as long as I could, holding on tight to my nose before exhaling all of my breath and letting the bubbles peck against my face. I thought about how it would be to die and thought this might be how it felt. A comforting but anxious feeling. All darkness and the sound of water. The thought of death was too much, though, and made a large, expanding feeling rise in my chest. I put my arms out and allowed myself to float back up.

Edie had jumped in, too, and as soon as I wiped the water from my eyes, she started splashing me. By the time we had been swimming for a few minutes, it seemed we were back to our old selves again. I suppose children are able to do that, although I'm not sure whether adults are. But I believe that Edie still thinks about the hot words I said to her that night. I certainly do. But that day we were just pleased to be swimming and together, and for a little while, at least, all was forgiven.

When our hands and feet were wrinkled from being in the water so long, we lay on the rocks and let the sun bake us. The sun broiled on the sky, a living thing that pulsated and grew larger. The heat bugs seemed to call out with the fury of the sun, screaming in the weeds lining the road. We lay there like dead people, our legs slightly apart, our arms straight down at our sides. If I had moved my little finger a half inch, it would have touched Edie's. We breathed in rhythm and didn't speak for a time, thinking only of how the sun felt on our wet skin.

After a while I got up and snatched the satchel from the limb. I made sure that my hands were completely dry and free of sand before I pulled the letters out of the sandwich bag.

"You shouldn't've done that," Edie said, sitting up. She held a hand at her brow, unused to the bright sun after having her eyes closed for so long, and looked down at the letters.

"She won't know," I said, but as these words escaped my mouth, I could picture my mother going into her bedroom and lifting the lid of her cedar box, peering in to find it half empty. Part of me thought my mother knew all things.

"It doesn't matter if she knows or not," Edie said. "It's not right. They're not yours to read."

"My daddy wrote them, didn't he?"

"He wrote them to *her*." Edie stood and grabbed her

shorts from the outcropping of limestone. She stepped into them with two hard stomps, then pulled her *Jaws* T-shirt over her high-necked green bathing suit. "Don't you feel bad?"

"It happened again, the night before last," I said.

"What?" she said, and leaned against a low-hanging branch from a mimosa tree that burst out of the riverbank.

"He had another nightmare. He hollered out in his sleep like someone was killing him."

"Did he do anything to Loretta?"

I shook my head. "But he jumped out of the bed and knocked everything off the dresser. He felt along the wall while he screamed and raked all the pictures off. Broke them. It took Mom and Nell both to get him calmed down."

"Well, reading them letters won't help you figure it out, Eli," she said. She was so sure of herself, so confident. I wished I could be like that, wished I could really feel that way deep down instead of just occasionally mustering up the strength to act as if I felt that way. "But I've got to go on home anyway," she said. "Daddy took off work today. I guess he wants the Father of the Year Award or something now."

She didn't leave, though. She stood there, looking down at me as I took one of the letters from its envelope. "He's taking me to the Tastee-Freez," she said at last. "You want to go?"

"Nah, you all should be alone."

"Yeah, I guess," she said, skipping a rock across the river. It glided along, touching down five times before sinking. "Why don't you come over later and watch *The Waltons* with me? And *Hawaii Five-O?*"

"I don't know. Mom likes for us to all watch *The Waltons* together."

"Well, I'll see you then," she said, quiet, looking away. Before I could say more, she had slid onto the path and was folded up by the woods. I had wanted her to at least stay with me while I read the letters. I didn't know what I might encounter. At the same time, I liked being alone with the letters. I held the flimsy stationery out from me so that the glints of sunlight on the river shone through the paper. It was so light and thin that if I had let go, the letter would have drifted away on the breath of air that was stirring. The pages would have separated reluctantly and winged just above the surface of the river, dipping and rolling over on itself, drifting away like a paper bird. So I held tight, my thumbs on one side, pressing onto my forefingers on the other side, and read:

29 April 1967
Dear Loretta,

Hey baby. It's the same old same old over here. Walk for days, hunker down and shoot it out awhile, go on night patrols. Same old. Our last hike lasted four days and I didn't take my boots off the whole time.

— *235*

When I finally did, my feet had changed completely. I looked down at them and couldn't believe they belonged to me. It's like my bones are knots. My toes are all scrunched up and laying atop one another. I asked for the medic to look at them and he just laughed. He said those were Vietnam feet and I was a real soldier now.

I don't even know what that means, to be a real soldier. This is really our war, though. You people back home don't know what it's all about but when you are here you get a different picture. You see, I am going to give these people over here my best even though it may mean my life. I've signed up and now I'll do my duty.

But I don't want to talk about the war or what's happening over here. I just want to think about you and Josie and the baby and the way home looks, the way the sky is smaller there. Remember that one time I took you up in the woods and showed you my old tree where I spent so much time as a boy? I hadn't been up there in years before I left home but I keep thinking about that little spot. In my dreams I am sitting beneath it and I can look up and see the wind passing through its leaves. Seems like I can even smell them woods in my dreams.

I have been taking lots of pictures of the trees over here. There is this one tree that I love in particular. Fruit grows everywhere on it, red and small like tommy toe tomatoes or cherries. Not just on the limbs, but even

on the trunk and the roots. It is a sight to behold. But
still it is not the trees back home.

In your next letter send me some more writing
paper because it is hard to get over here. I can't get it,
period, to tell the truth. And envelopes. And some new
pictures if you can. Little ones so I can carry them easy.
That's all that gets me through the day, my picture of
you three. I better go and save my light. Write me when
you can, and when you pray, pray for me. I'll see you
very soon, darling. Until then, you have my love.

Always,
Stanton Book

On this one he had signed his last name, which I thought
strange. By that time they had been married six years. But
maybe he was trying to hold on to himself. I thought that
maybe he repeated his own name to himself over and over,
the way he had once said my mother's name—Loretta
Loretta Loretta—in a sort of prayer to save himself.

My Dearest Dear,
Do you remember that song, "My Dearest Dear"?
My mother and Nell used to sit on the porch and sing it
in the cool of the day. Sometimes I hum it to myself
because I can't remember all the words but I always
think of you because you are surely my dearest dear.

I can hear my mother and Nell singing that just as

plain as day, just like I am back on that porch. It don't pay to study on old times, though, so I'll move on.

    I have to write this down to make it real, although I do not want to. This letter will be short as I don't know how much I can bear to write. My best friend was killed last night. We were out patrolling this big rice paddy that went on for ages, a field that seemed big as the world to me. The worst thunderstorm I've ever seen. Storms over here are a thing to behold. When one comes up it seems like the whole world is ending. He was there, right beside me. And then a bolt of lightning come down like it had been hunting him and struck him right in the top of the head. He fell down beside me and it looked like there wasn't a thing wrong with him. I had always heard that lightning will burn you up or at least burn your clothes off. And I had heard you weren't supposed to touch a person who had been hit with lightning or you'd be shocked, too. But I didn't think of that — I just grabbed hold of him. I didn't feel anything. He looked just fine except that his eyes were rolled back in his head and when I shook him he didn't even flinch and before long I realized that he was solid dead. I carried him on my back. A person is awful heavy when the life is gone from them, especially in that wet field. It was like walking through concrete with that rice paddy up to my knees almost.

    I don't want to go on about it. His name was Larry

Caudill. He was 21 years old. A good way to go, I guess, although a person don't expect to come to a war and be killed by nature. You'd think that's the last thing that would get you in a place that doesn't even seem real.
 Thinking of you always,
 Stanton Book

And then two letters where he asked for more paper, where he talked about missing home, the trees, Josie's laughter. In all the letters he was holding back, not saying all he wanted to. Even a ten-year-old could see that. Maybe he couldn't bear to write it all down. But in each one, there is something else that is left unsaid. The lines of the letters are like waves on the middle of the ocean, each of them covering a whole world beneath.

In one he said that I was eight months and two days old and he had never laid eyes on me. *I will make it up to him someday, not being there. When I can I'll be with him every minute of the day,* he had written. That hadn't worked out like he had wanted, because when he got home he worked most all the time, fixing something on his truck or mowing the yard or breaking up the garden. I suppose he had tried his best to be one of those fathers who is always there, tossing a baseball and all that, but he wasn't, and I was okay with that. I knew that he had to work, and that was all right. The problem was how quiet he was with me most of the time, the way he hardly ever noticed me. The last time I had felt like he was truly mine was when he had left me drive to the gas station, more than a month ago. I remembered the way he had kissed the back of my head.

And then, this letter, which was the last one of his I ever read:

> . . . *I felt the shrapnel tear into my back but I couldn't even take the time to put my fingers to the torn places in my skin because I had to do what needed done. I have to tell you, Loretta, that I was scared to death. I've seen a lot over here that I'll never be able to work my mind around properly but this time I felt terror. I know what that's like now, and I can admit that. It helps to admit it. You see everything in flashes, like a fast slide-show. You can feel the blood in your veins and you can remember everything about your life and all that is in your head but at the same time you are only thinking of pulling the trigger, of surviving. It's a funny thing, the way your mind works, the way survival takes over. All I can do is count the days until I am gone from this place and this lousy army. I close my eyes to go to sleep at night and I relive it all. The thing is that I accepted death, Loretta. I was certain that I would never see the light of day again. But I am here.*
>
> *Love, as always, yours,*
> *Stanton Book*

There was something about this particular letter that got to me in a way no other had. Maybe it was everything that he wasn't saying. Or maybe he was too much like a real person to me, something we don't think of our parents being until we are much older. When I finished reading it, I found that my breath was heavy, as if I had been running a long time. I should never have read those letters at my age. It was too much for a child to properly digest.

The next envelope was blank and much heavier than the others, and I could tell right away that it contained a few pictures. Seven of them, all in color except for one:

1. A little boy in a long-sleeved, pin-striped shirt, smoking a cigarette with a small smile. A younger boy stands beside him, thumbs and forefingers together at his belly, looking into the camera. A hut and palm trees behind them. The inscription on the back reads: *Ton and Tin, Phuoc Vinh.*

2. My father, shirtless, holding what looks like a machine gun with a wooden stock. He doesn't look as old as Charles Asher, except in the eyes. He and another man (who wears black plastic glasses and has a wet rag around his neck) are looking up into what resembles a persimmon tree. There is a monkey sitting within the crook of two branches, and he looks like he's laughing. The man with glasses is laughing, too, but my father is not. On the back my father has printed: *Me, Robinson, and our monkey, Woody.*

3. A dirt road, palm trees on either side. A white sky. I

have to squint to see, but it is undeniable: there are twelve dead bodies lying in the road. One of them is almost completely red with blood. One tire of a jeep is visible in the lower left corner. At the far end of the road there is a green tank with a large white star on its side. I don't notice for a long time that there are several American soldiers standing near the bodies, looking down at them, as frozen as the corpses. I studied this one a long time. There is no writing on the back.

4. A dark-skinned man sits on the ground with a cloth bag over his face. The picture is full of movement — I can imagine his head darting about, trying to figure out the sounds around him — except for my father, who is standing very still in this photo, too. He is looking away from the hostage, far out over the fields, which are brown and yellow and dead. There is no writing on the back.

5. Here is one of my father wearing a green uniform, high black lace-up boots, a helmet. He is standing next to a briar patch covered in purple-pink blooms that look like wild roses. He has snatched one of the flowers off and put it between his ear and helmet. On the back: *I had Caudill take this picture of me because I thought you'd like the flowers. A little bit of beauty here in hell.*

6. Six big helicopters sitting in a field. Their blades are a blur of motion, cutting the picture in two. The sky is low and gray, the color of an old spoon. No inscription on the back.

7. My father cutting a boy's hair. A towel is spread out

over the boy's shoulders and covers him to the waist, where green soldier pants show. My father's hand is spread out completely flat on the top of the soldier's head and he is looking very intently at the small scissors in his hands as he snips away hair. The boy's head is bent down but he has brought his eyes up to meet the camera, one brow arched. Behind them there is a thickness of woods. This is the only picture that is in black-and-white, and on the back my father wrote: *Cutting Caudill's hair. He's my best friend over here.*

I didn't want to take too much time to think about what I had seen and read, so I put the pictures back into their envelope and arranged them all neatly in the sandwich bag and placed them in the canvas satchel. I had been sitting there so long that my hair had dried and my shorts were only damp. The sun burned through the trees with such a white fierceness that I could almost hear the leaves crisping on the limbs. The heat bugs clicked in the grass. It was now the middle of July and it hadn't rained since I had stood out in that thunderstorm and nearly scared Daddy to death. I didn't want to think about how I might have caused him to start having his flashbacks, which is what Josie called them. She had gone to the library and looked up a bunch of books about veterans. She had lain down on the bed beside me and run her long finger down the page, trying to explain things to me.

"The vets from Vietnam have it worse because they were flown straight home," she had said. I had watched her as she looked at the words on the page. I had no idea what she was talking about, but then she explained. "In the Second World War, the men had to take this real long boat ride back home, but soldiers like Daddy were in Vietnam one day and back home the next. They didn't have time to think it all through before they got back to their people, so it's worse for them."

I meandered through the woods and found my bicycle lying at the end of the path, beside the road. I pumped my legs hard down the dusty road, thinking of nothing, focused completely on driving the bicycle as fast as I could. I was suddenly panicked and felt that if I didn't get the letters back home and properly hidden in the cedar box, I would surely be found out. Besides, I didn't want them in my possession anymore.

TWENTY-FOUR

Josie was a storm that moved through the house. She stomped away from our mother, who was right at her heels, her face stretched tight with anger. Josie slammed her bedroom door, slid past where Loretta was yelling in the hallway, and whirled around on one heel to face her. As she did so, she jerked at the back of a kitchen chair too hard and sent it straight to the floor, its back making a high crack on the still, hot air of the house.

Josie had on her flag pants, and this time Mom wasn't going to back down. I stood in the back door, watching them, although I don't think they had even noticed my entrance. I had my satchel strapped over my shoulder and was torn on what I should do. This fight was occupying Mom in such a way that I had the perfect opportunity to return the letters to the cedar box without her noticing. But I hated to miss this fight, because it was going to be a big one. A part of me was thrilled by their arguing, so I wanted to see it for the entertainment value. Another part of me hated to see them so mad at each other, so I wanted to stay and intervene if the need arose.

"Take them off right now!" My mother thrust a finger into the air, toward the pants. "Right this minute."

Josie looked completely taken aback, as if someone had just told her to put a gun to her temple and pull the trigger. "I *won't!*" she screamed. "After what you did, you don't have no right to make me do anything!"

Mom took one step forward, a giant step, like someone bobbing over a narrow creek, and wrapped her hand around Josie's wrist. She brought her face down close to Josie's, their eyes burning into each other's. "This is one time that you're going to mind me, Josie Michelle. You are going to take those pants off and I'm going to throw them away and then you're going to your room for the rest of the night."

"Charles Asher is coming to get me," she yelled, appalled. She tried to peel Mom's fingers away from her arm, but it did no good. Our mother was not going to back down this time.

"You're not going anywhere with Charles Asher," Mom said. "I know what you've been doing with him, and this is going to stop now. You're going to take off those pants right this minute. And you're going to stop running wild."

"What am I doing with him, Mom?"

Quieter now: "You know what I mean, Josie. Don't make me say it in front of Eli."

So they did know I was there.

"We're not doing anything you didn't do," Josie said. She was enjoying this. The words spewed from her like someone caught up in a fire-and-brimstone campaign speech. "But I'm smarter than you."

Mom ripped her hand away from Josie's wrist, and Josie stepped back, touching her arm as if she were hurt. Then Mom unleashed her anger on me instead of Josie. She whirled around and faced me, her sharp finger pointing toward the door, her words urgent and high. "Go back outside, Eli!" she hollered. "I'm tired of your spying! *Right now!*"

Although my mother had never screamed at me this way before, I only scrambled out onto the screen porch and cowered near the back door, where I could still hear them. Mom was so caught up in all the words that she didn't even notice when I peeked around the door frame.

"How dare you speak to me that way, Josie," she said, calmer now. She seemed to measure out each word.

"How dare *you* lie to me," Josie said, her hands balled into fists. "And how dare *you* act so high and mighty. Do you realize what a terrible mother you've been to both of us? Lying to me, *never* there for Eli."

"Never there?"

"Always caught up in some la-la land with Daddy, worshipping him —"

"You ought to be glad your parents love each other. What if you had parents like Edie?"

"But you always loved him more than us," Josie said. Even though I had felt this way many times, I knew that Josie didn't really believe anything she was saying. She was just throwing gas on a raging fire. "You always chose him over us. I *despise* you."

My mother said nothing. I looked around the door frame and saw her there with her back to me, her shoulders slumped, yet rising with each deep breath she took. She was shaking her head no, slowly back and forth.

"And it's because Daddy *saved* you, you think," Josie said, mocking. Her eyes were wild, huge. "Because I wouldn't have had a father otherwise, right? If you hadn't been running wild, maybe you wouldn't have got knocked up with me," Josie said, a smile creeping out over her lips. "I'm not a slut like you were."

My mother sliced her hand through the air and slapped Josie's face. The sound was sharp and piercing, like someone bringing a book down hard on a table. Worse than the sound was the way Josie looked, though. Her face was taken over by a scowl of disbelief and complete belief, all tangled up in one open-mouthed gasp. She put her trembling fingertips against the place where Mom had hit her and brought her hand out to look at them, as if blood might be there.

Josie drew her face tight, and just as her gathered mouth and fretted brow let me know what she was about to do, she threw her hand up and slapped our mother.

Her impact was less open-handed and produced a dull thud against Mom's cheek, but she had hit her own mother in the face, and this was too much. This had gone too far. I stepped forward, wanting to do something, to say something, but there was nothing to say. I couldn't understand where Nell had run off to. She could have stepped in and said the right thing and stopped all of this. Peacemakers were never around when they were needed, I decided. They showed up only after the war was already in progress.

And then I realized that my father was standing in the back doorway, stopped in his tracks between the kitchen and the screen porch. He had walked up just as Josie's blow had landed on Mom's face. He had been holding his metal lunchbox in one hand and his Thermos in the other, but he dropped both of them at the same time and they hit the floor — the lunchbox a muted clatter, the Thermos a dark thud.

He bolted across the room and grabbed Josie by the

wrist. She struggled around, her hair thrashing about. Her voice was small and clipped: "Please" and "Daddy" and "Don't." But he paid no attention to her. He pulled her out onto the porch, threw open the screen door, and then they tumbled off the steps and into the yard. He was a ghost of himself, his eyes gone dead again, his face drawn up into that war look.

My mother and I were close behind. Once, when Josie was thrashing about, she came around to face me and two little breaths pumped out of her mouth: "Eli." As if there was anything I could do to save her. But her eyes were looking at me as if to warn me, as if to say, "Run!" Maybe if I said "Daddy" in a small voice, the way I had that night when he was strangling my mother, he would snap out of it. But I didn't think so. It didn't even seem like I should try. Besides, Josie had slapped Mom. She deserved punishment. Still, though, Daddy had never spanked either of us that I could remember. Mom always did that. And wasn't Josie too old to spank, anyway? I didn't know what he was going to do. He stood there on the yard with Josie twisting around at the end of his arm like a huge, disobeying fish that didn't want to be taken off the hook. She was a little girl now, terrified, begging him to let her go. And what was terrifying was that our father's face had been overtaken by the war again. He wasn't even there anymore, so we couldn't predict his movements.

Mom put her hands out to Daddy, her eyes full of kindness and heartbreak. "Stanton," she said, a coo. "Let her go. I'll take care of it."

At last Josie wrestled free. In her fright, off balance, she fell onto the yard, flat on her rump. She was too scared or shocked to move. She sat there with both hands on the ground on either side of her. Her hair hung down in her face, and long lines of it puffed in and out when she breathed. Only one of her eyes showed through the wild black mane.

"You slapped your mother," Daddy said, amazingly calm, as if he had collected himself in the struggle to get outside. He stood over her with his hands on his hips.

"She slapped me first," Josie said.

"Why?" Daddy said.

Josie put one hand up to her face and pushed her hair aside, hooking it behind her right ear. Her lower lip was trembling. Her face showed everything that was going through her mind: terror, defiance, sadness, anger. All these things played across her forehead and her eyes, in the way she held her mouth and managed to stop the trembling.

"Answer me!" he boomed. I saw then that he was breathing hard, too. Josie had given him a run for his money. Maybe her wild spirit had impressed him, had made him realize what he was about to do. Because it had looked as if he was going to get her out onto the yard and take his belt to her, but now he was listening. I didn't want Josie to be in trouble, but I also wanted her to be set straight, once and for all. I was tired of her drama.

Josie pressed her hands against the ground and sprang up. She looked very tall and beautiful and grown. She wasn't scared of anything anymore. "Why didn't you tell me that I wasn't your child sooner?"

I sat down on the steps. I wasn't sure if I wanted to eavesdrop on all this or not.

"Because it didn't matter," Daddy said, becoming himself again, his face easing out. Quiet, but forceful, too. Each word a firmness. "Because you've always been my child, no matter what. I've never thought of you as anything less than my own child."

"But I'm *not*," Josie said, her hands cupped out in front of her, as if waiting to receive something solid and real instead of words. "I have a father out there somewhere, and you shouldn't have hid that from me. I'm sixteen years old."

Our mother took a step forward. "And when you turned sixteen, I told you."

"You should've told me earlier," Josie said, and looked away. She closed her eyes for a short time, breathing in the summer air, letting it fill her. "It's my life, my *history*."

"For the last couple of years you've been angry just for the sake of being angry, anyway," Mom said.

"Wouldn't you be?" Josie said, looking up as if startled.

"Even before all this, though," Mom said. "Your generation doesn't have anything to be mad about, so y'all are mad about *everything*." Her words became quick little blocks now. "So I want you to go in the house and pull those pants off and end this foolishness."

"Is that what this is all about?" Daddy said, as if he hadn't even noticed the flag pants before.

My mother nodded. "It's not right, her wearing them after you fought for this country —"

"That don't matter," Daddy said, cutting her off.

Josie stood before him, her elbows cupped in her hands. She massaged her elbows as if they had been harmed in their skirmish, looking at the ground.

"Josie," he said. Her name sounded so tender coming from him, as if all his pain and sorrow were wrapped up in those two syllables. "Haven't I been a good daddy to you? Haven't I done everything for you?"

Josie paused, then nodded, two short bobs of her head.

"Are you mad at me about Vietnam?" he said, his voice full of expectation. "About me fighting in the war? Is that what you're mad about?"

Josie seemed taken aback. When she answered — "No" — the word was nothing more than a curled exhalation of breath.

Daddy stepped forward and put his hand on Josie's arm. She looked up at him as if she had no idea what he was about to do. I didn't, either.

"The way you talk about everything — always saying all war is wrong, talking about all that history none of us can help. It's like you're saying it all to me. Don't you know that I fought for this country?"

Each word rose in urgency, and I was convinced that he was out of his mind now. He never said so much all at once.

I had been mistaken; the war hadn't left him. He hadn't calmed at all. He had been like a kettle of water that boils before you realize it, and now he was at full boil again. The war slid right back down his body as if he were stepping into a new set of clothes. His hand was tightening on her arm; she began to twist under the grasp.

"You stand there and cry about not belonging to me. Don't you realize that when I was over there — killing for my country — I was really killing for you, for Eli?"

Josie tried to pull away. She kept twisting, but she couldn't get out of his grip. "Daddy, please," she said.

"You think you have it all figured out and you don't know *shit,*" he said, little specks of spit spraying from his mouth. Angry now, his whole body changing, becoming larger and more solid. "I'm always listening to you, Josie. When you say you hate this country, you're saying that you hate me."

"I don't know what you mean." Josie said each word separately, searching for the next word without knowing what she actually wanted to say. "I don't hate it. That's not what I mean." Screwing her face up into a mask of confusion. It seemed that our father had melted down inside this man talking here on the yard, that he had been overtaken by someone else. He had lost his mind.

"Stanton," Mom said, "what are you talking about?"

He held on to Josie's arms, staring into her face as if he wanted to memorize her, then his whole face contorted and he started yelling. "You. Don't. Know!" he screamed, shaking her so hard that her hair snapped out behind her and slapped her back.

Then Mom was pulling at him, saying his name over and over, the way he had repeated her name while in Vietnam, but this time it wasn't a prayer. It was a pleading.

I thought he was going to shake the life out of Josie. I thought he'd break her neck. And then he released her only long enough to grab her face within both of his big hands. He cupped her cheeks, bringing himself closer to her, looking her right in the eye, his own eyes gone, dead, black.

"You shouldn't," he said, a ghost.

My mother was at his back, hollering his name over and over, as if it were the only word she knew how to say.

All I could see was her face, scrunched up into that look of complete terror and disbelief. I knew how she felt; I had been there before. So I had to do something.

I raced up behind Daddy and hit him as hard as I could in the small of his back. This didn't faze him, so I ran around and scurried up his leg just enough to sink my fingernails into his face. I tugged my hand down. I could feel his skin peeling away, glanced at the two little lines of thin blood that were appearing on his cheek. His hand came out, nothing more than a reaction, really, and slapped me away. His knuckles caught me across the bridge of my nose, so that I actually saw stars for one smarting second. Then I fell to the ground, face-first, although I didn't feel anything.

I thought I heard my mother cry out "No!" but I couldn't be sure.

I wasn't even aware of scrambling up and standing again, but by the time I had, everyone had grown completely still.

Daddy stood before me, taking in great breaths of air. Mom stood near him, but her eyes touched mine. He was still hanging on to Josie, but after what seemed a long time of us all looking at one another — everyone's breathing filling the quiet — he pushed her away and she dropped onto the grass near me. She fell into a heap there, her legs out beside her, leaning on one arm, crying into her other hand.

Daddy turned and sauntered away. He disappeared around the corner of the house, and then we heard the engine of his truck firing up. He sped out of the driveway, and then the sound of his truck was gone, lost to the thick summer air.

"Go pull them off," Mom said to Josie, sounding as if her mouth were full of dirt. "Right now." As Josie stomped into the house, Mom crumbled down onto the grass before me, her skirt riding high up above her knees. She took the sides of my face in her hands, turning my head this way and that to look over my injuries.

"There's no marks on you," she said, speaking quick, as

if she might not have time to say everything she wanted to. "See, now? Look. You're fine. He didn't mean it, baby." Her eyes darted here and there, trying to cover every square inch of my face. "Are you hurt?"

I shook my head no.

The gloaming began to settle around us there on the yard, the air pulsating with a purpling light that smoothed out the edges of the world. Everything became very quiet, and a cool curtain — not a breeze; more like a wall of air — moved past us. I looked up to the ridge, feeling animal eyes upon me. I thought the little fox might be observing all this and trying to figure out what had just happened. But a child-fox would have been grown by now. Born in the spring, he would have already left childish things behind.

After a time she spoke toward the ground. "Do you know where Nell is?"

"Probably went walking by the river."

"Go find her."

TWENTY-FIVE

My legs were filled with an urgency I didn't completely understand. Maybe I knew that I had to hurry and find Nell before the gloaming seeped away and night overtook the world. Perhaps I thought that, somehow, Nell would be able to fix everything. I didn't completely understand what had happened between my father and Josie anyway, and Nell always helped to put things into perspective for me. But maybe a part of me knew that my father had completely lost it, that he was heading for a breakdown. A part of me even knew what I was about to find.

I pumped the pedals of the bicycle the way I did when I raced Edie down this same stretch of road in the mornings, when the mist was breathing out of the hillsides. I rode past Stella's and she called out to me — "Where are you going in such a hurry?" — as she watered the flowers on her front porch, but I didn't even acknowledge her. Then past the old couple who always worked in their gardens in the cool of the day. They glanced up at me, then back to their hoeing. And then to the part of the road where the woods took over, dark green leaves making a roof over me. Here it was cooler, almost autumn-smelling, and especially quiet. There were no night sounds yet; the cicadas and crickets seemed to rest up during twilight.

I didn't know if I was searching for Nell or my father. But I found them both at the high bridge where the little boy had died, where Daddy had paused that day on the way to the station. Daddy's truck was stopped right in the middle of the bridge, the driver's door open. If another car had come racing down the road from the opposite direction, it would have torn the door right off, as the bridge was narrow and long.

My father was standing on the bridge's concrete railing, balancing himself there like a tightrope walker as he looked down at the place where the river began to rush and turn white with speed. His arms were down at his sides, and his face was peaceful, accepting. There was something like hope and something like despair all mixed up in his eyes. Nell was running up the road on the other side of the bridge, her mouth opening to holler. I stopped as soon as I saw him and stood with my legs planted firmly on either side of my bicycle. I didn't know what to do. Approaching him might make him jump. If I stood there and didn't move, I would watch him take one beautiful step off into the air and fall straight down and I'd blame myself forever.

"Stanton!" I heard Nell's scream, which sounded as if it had been ripped up out of the bottom of her ribs. She was running faster, her hands curled up into fists that punched at the air as she ran. Her bell-bottoms sailed like flags around her calves, and her peasant blouse rode up, exposing her white belly. She had plaited her hair, and the braid trailed out behind her like a horse's tightly woven tail. Her broad, smart forehead was even wider than usual. "Please!"

I walked my bicycle a little closer, still straddling the bar that ran from handlebars to seat. I thought about turning around and riding away. I didn't want to see my father commit suicide. But it felt wrong to leave, too. I moved onto the edge of the woods and let my bicycle fall to the ground. I squatted down beside it.

I didn't dare get too close, though. I thought he might see me out of the corner of his eye and be so ashamed that he would go ahead and step off.

I felt what he felt when he stood there. I believed that at the time, anyway. I imagined what was going through his mind.

Rain on big leaves.

Lightning that came down and touched the top of his best friend's head.

The soldier he killed, the way he crumpled down and his hand stretched out, his fingers uncurling and letting go of the gun, my father standing over him and seeing that he was just a person, imagining that the man had children and a family and a home somewhere at the end of a jungle path.

All the faceless men whose hearts were stopped by bullets fired from his machine gun. He saw all of them when he slept at night and gave each of them faces.

Children lining the road, dressed in long sleeves beneath the broiling sun, their hands out. My father placing halves of Hershey bars there.

Thinking of me and Josie when he looked into their eyes.

Thinking of these children's dead fathers or mothers he had seen lying near the huts.

Rows of men marching through rice paddies, their rifles drawn.

The hostage they kept in the field, with men at four corners, watching the night.

The way the shrapnel bit into his back like shards of glass.

The gunfire and mortars and all the explosions bursting as if he were floating in the sky among a collection of July fireworks instead of lying on foreign land with his face pressed close to the ground.

A field full of dead men, men he knew.

The whir of helicopter blades.

The explosions, the planes that flew very low and let down a rain of napalm that burned up the trees.

And all the trees, the beautiful trees that would always remember his hand upon their trunks as he passed them on his long walks across a country he did not know.

He saw himself strutting down the streets of Boston, a free man now, a survivor.

And two girls spitting at his feet.

"Baby-killer," they said. Moving through the world like a dream.

Nell was not one to stand back and watch. She ran right up to the bridge railing and put her hands on his ankles. "Stanton, please, God," she said. They hadn't really spoken since that night he destroyed the guitar. She gripped his ankles as if she could keep him from jumping this way.

"Go on, Nell," he said, words spoken by the living dead.

Again I thought my calling out to him the way I had done that night in their bedroom might solve everything. But I was afraid to speak. I was afraid the breath expelled by my voice would swirl through the air and punch him in the small of the back, causing him to fall.

"It's all right," Nell said. She had collected herself now and had let go of his ankles. She wiped at her face with the backs of both hands, then held on to the railing. She felt her way down the railing so that she could come to his side and look up at him. He kept his eyes on the river. "Think of Eli and Josie. And Loretta. And me. Don't you know how much we all worship you?"

"It don't matter," he said, just as he had said to my mother about the flag pants. Nothing mattered, that's what he was saying. "I've lost them. I've lost everything."

"No," Nell said, speaking quickly, shaking her head. "Look at what all you've gained since you came back from there. Your own little house and your children and your wife. The station and all the people who look up to you and respect you."

"I keep seeing that man's face," he said.

"You chose life," Nell said. "Choose it now, Stanton. Don't do this to your family. It's too selfish, and that's one thing you've never, ever been."

He looked at her, jerking his head around as if she had said something insulting.

"Don't you know how much I loved you?" she said. Her voice shuddered, like someone who has been crying long and hard. There were no tears in her eyes, but her face and voice were full of grieving. She curled in on herself, trembling. She had to keep her brother from killing himself and she knew it. "Can't you see that that's why I was out there protesting? It was all for you."

I crawled closer on my hands and knees, easing along the side of the road in the higher grass and tiger lilies.

Daddy had kept his eyes on Nell the whole time she

spoke, but now he turned back to the river. "I could float down and be lost forever," he said, like a poem. Like a grown man standing in a classroom, reading a poem aloud for his teacher. "I could."

"Step down from there to me, Stanton," Nell said, and put her hand on the back of his calf. I thought about the line from that book she had read me at the beginning of the summer: *Only the rocks live forever.* She spread her whole palm out there. "Remember when you were little and would have growing pains? I'd set for an hour and rub your legs. I'd do anything for you when you's little. I still would. My little brother. I always—" At this she couldn't contain her grief anymore, her face convulsed with weeping.

"Go on, Nell," he said again, not wanting to think about all that, not wanting to let the good creep in.

"I'm the one who's supposed to be dying," she said, and laughed like a crazy person through her tears. "I have to go first."

I stood and clung behind a small beech that stood near the road. If I leaned out just enough, I could see them.

Nell put her hand out to him and stood that way a long time, peering up at him, not letting her eyes leave his face. He ignored her hand but she stood right there without moving. I don't know how she held her arm up that long.

The gloaming had moved on, slipped back up into the sky, and darkness was taking over the valley now. The moon was a white rind above the horizon. One by one the crickets began to call out. Some kind of insect sounded every few minutes, like a tambourine being shaken.

I thought we might be there forever, three people stuck in time.

And then, all at once, he simply put out his hand and took hers. He stepped off the bridge railing as easily as someone coming off a porch step. They didn't embrace, but he put his arm around her back as they walked toward the truck. He leaned on her like a man with a broken leg. Neither of them spoke.

But then he saw me. I just stood there, feeling an overwhelming sense of sadness wash over me. I had felt alone all of my life, had felt as if my parents only saw each other as they moved through the world, thought they loved each other so much that there was no room to love me. But now, by the way Daddy looked at me, I knew better.

His face is what convinced me. He was so hurt to see me there, to know I had seen all of this. So I knew, once and for all, that he did care if I existed or not.

Daddy walked toward me with his hands out in front of him, his steps picking up speed until he was in a little sprint. When he reached me, he capped his hand around the back of my head and pulled my face into the oily scent of his work shirt, against his belly.

"Oh, God. I'm sorry, buddy," he said. "I didn't know you was there."

I put my arms around his waist. I drew in the scent of

the service station that was held within the fabric of his shirt, gas and grease and the cool contained in the shadows of the cement-block garage.

I felt worn out, the same way I had felt the night of the fireworks when all the excitement of the Fourth mixed with my regret over the argument with Edie had completely exhausted me. I suppose my father sensed this, so he picked me up. He placed me in the crook of his right arm, against his hip, and with his left arm he picked up the bicycle, hooking it over his left arm. I laid my head on his shoulder while Nell stood by the truck, watching us.

We bounced back over the rough road toward home. I sat between them, but closer to my father. Not a one of us spoke. I had never been in his truck before when the radio wasn't playing, but now it was silent, and I listened to the warm grind of the motor, the way the gearshift clicked in a silver sound every time we went over a bump, the redundant sound of the wind searching through the sheaf of papers my father kept tucked behind the visor hanging over his seat. Daddy kept both hands on the steering wheel, his eyes following the yellow headlights, but his side was open and warm to me, so I cowered there against him.

TWENTY-SIX

I don't believe my mother ever knew how close my father came to jumping off that bridge. I certainly never told her, and I can't imagine that Nell or Daddy did, either. Maybe he did; they often had long, serious talks when they lay down at night. But somehow I think he knew better than to give her this awful knowledge. She would have been forever worried, even after he finally sought out help later that year. The only time I ever mentioned it was that very night, when I told Josie.

Late that night, I finished Anne Frank's diary, and I wanted to go over and peck on Edie's window and let her know that it was now one of my all-time favorites. She had been anxious for me to be done with the book so we could talk about it. Finding out that Anne had died that way, after all that hope and happiness she carried around throughout the book, was almost too much to bear, and I needed to talk to Edie about it, mostly because I didn't completely understand the way the book had made me feel. I knew that Anne was dead, yet I felt hopeful. That reaction didn't make any sense.

It was past midnight, so I was easing out the back door when I noticed Josie sitting on the glider — in Nell's regular spot — completely still.

"Where do you think you're going?" she said, a little laugh in her voice.

"Over to Edie's."

"This late? Her daddy will shoot you one of these days." She patted the glider seat beside her. "Come talk to me a minute. You're always off in the woods or somewhere. You used to always be on my heels."

I sat down and she stretched her arm across my shoulders. "You're always with Charles Asher or gone," I said. "Or mad."

"Well, the Charles Asher part won't be a problem anymore. We broke up tonight."

A wash of regret ran down into my belly. "Why'd you do that? I *knew* you'd do that someday."

She laughed. "Well, it wasn't up to me. He broke up with me."

"No *way,*" I said. This was unbelievable. Everybody knew that he was crazy about her.

"He did," she said. "But it's all right; I'll make it."

Everybody was always talking to me like I was older, like I was their *confidante* (another word that Edie had looked up in her dictionary and tried to use as much as possible — she had once told me that her confidante was the willow tree).

"You were awful to him all the time," I said. I hated the thought of Charles Asher not being at the house with us anymore.

"I know," she said, as if speaking to herself, and looked out at the yard.

"You've been mad all the time lately," I told her, and she didn't say anything, just kept looking out at the darkness like something was moving about out there, something only she could hear. I looked down at her hand, lying there on her lap. Her fingernails were chewed down, the white polish chipped and worn. This made me real sorry for her, but I was still mad at her, too. She was six years older than me, and I thought she was grown, that she had everything figured out. But somehow I also knew that I understood more than she did.

A brief wind slithered through the porch, a sign of oncoming rain. The wind chimes clicked together in the corner, and the night was so still and black that I could hear the corn rustling out in Mom and Stella's garden.

"Daddy almost jumped off the bridge tonight," I announced.

She might as well have said "What?" in a shocked way, because I felt this question in the sudden stiffening of her body beside me. She looked at me, and when I didn't reply for a time, she squeezed my shoulder with her hand. "What are you talking about?"

And so I told her. She listened without interrupting me, but her face replied in all the right places. When I was finished, she leaned over and kissed me. I wondered if her pink lipstick had left a mark on my forehead.

"It'll be all right," she said. "Don't worry so much, okay? You're too little to be worrying all the time."

We sat in silence for a time, not moving or speaking, then I went into the house and lay down on the floor so I could pull the yellow Whitman's Sampler box out from under my bed. I had not had a chance to return the last batch of letters to Mom's cedar box, since I had come home to find Mom and Josie in their big fight and hadn't been able to get into the bedroom. After finding Daddy at the bridge, I hadn't even thought of them again until Mom was already in bed. Now I was glad that I had not had the chance because it was time that Josie saw how Daddy had always been thinking of her while he was in Vietnam. I sat very close to her while she read the letters, pointing out lines where he mentioned her, remembered her, asked about her. She read the letters without speaking, occasionally letting out a little laugh that sounded like pure joy to me, tensing up and not speaking on the worst parts.

It was very late by the time she had read the letters and looked at the pictures. She didn't say that I shouldn't have stolen these items of our parents' history. She only looked at me for a time with thanks spelled out in her eyes.

After a while she got up and unfolded the camping cot that stood in the corner of the porch. "Let's sleep out here tonight," she said. "Want to? We haven't done that in ages."

She didn't wait for me to reply before she went into the house to get me some pillows and covers to make a pallet. I would wait until tomorrow to tell Edie how I felt about Anne Frank. Then I realized what comforted me about the book: even though Anne Frank was dead now, it was even bigger that someone as strong and brave as she was had once lived. That was enough. She had been a child of war, like me, but she made sure that she was more than that. I had to do the same.

TWENTY-SEVEN

One morning Nell awoke and decided it was time to move on.

That's the way she operated, my mother said. "She's a gypsy, always has been."

I was devastated, of course. I couldn't imagine the rest of my life without her on that screen porch, without finding the pitcher of sweet tea she had left out on the counter, the empty toilet-paper roll she had failed to refill, the sound of her songs playing on her little green record player sitting in the grass. I kept thinking that she was leaving so she could go off and die of cancer. So I was terrified. And I was mad.

But there was no changing her mind. She packed, biting on the end of a cigarette that sent smoke washing up over her eyes, while I sat on the bed, watching.

"You go back to school in two days, anyway," she said. "You won't even miss me once you get back in class."

She made me sit on her suitcase so she could click the brass latches, then tousled my hair and put her palm flat against my forehead, pushing me back onto the bed, where she was able to tickle me until I nearly peed on myself. The cigarette remained clamped between her teeth the entire time as she laughed.

Then she allowed me to sit up, and she produced a double-record album. *The White Album* by the Beatles.

"Some of the songs on there might freak Loretta out, so don't play it too loud," she said, her face very serious, as if she was giving me instructions of proper living. "But 'Blackbird' is on there, and 'Mother Nature's Son.' And 'Rocky Raccoon'—you love that one."

"And 'Bungalow Bill'?"

She nodded. "And 'While My Guitar Gently Weeps.' All the best ones."

I gave her my copy of *Anne Frank: The Diary of a Young Girl*. She sat down and ran her palm over its cool cover. "What a beautiful gift," she said. "There's no better present than a book."

More than anything, I would miss looking at the cover; Anne Frank's good face looking out at me over the years, her eyes saying *I am here* just as clearly as the trees always did. "It's sad, though," I offered. "It's about a little girl in World War II."

"I know," she said. She dropped her cigarette into the half-inch of Dr Pepper that remained in my bottle. Mom hated when Nell did this, but she always washed the bottles out without saying anything. "It was one of my favorites when I was little. But I don't have my own copy, so I can't thank you enough."

I knew that I was about to cry, but I didn't know that it was showing on my face until I felt my lip trembling.

"Eli? What is it?" Nell said, touching my face. "What's wrong?"

"I know about you having cancer," I stammered. "I'm afraid I'll never see you again."

"Oh, God," she said, and pulled me to her. "It's all right. Hush, now. Hush."

We sat like that for a time. Then she held me out in front of her by the shoulders. "I am not going to die, Eli Book. You mark my words. It'll take more than cancer to get me down."

"But it's bad," I said. "I heard you tell Daddy."

"Yes, it's bad. But so am I."

I knew she wanted me to laugh, but I couldn't, even though I did believe her. She was too strong, too fierce, too alive. It would be much later before I overheard my parents talking about how she had come home to die but had decided to fight it harder instead. I liked to think that being with all of us caused her to want to live more than she had before.

Nell stood and clapped her hands together as if we should move on. She snatched up a box of books that had her green record player sitting atop it. "Get my suitcase," she said, and stomped out of the room as if carrying a great load.

My mother had just loaded a box of albums into the truck and met us at the back door. Josie sat on the porch glider, distraught. Daddy was standing out on the yard, bathed in a crimson light that caused him to look much older than he was. He was peering out at the garden as if something there held great interest. I watched him while Nell hugged Josie and put her thumbs into the corners of Josie's eyes, wiping outward. She told her to quit acting foolish; she'd see her soon. I wonder now if Josie was privy to the knowledge of Nell's cancer. She was crying with such devotion that she must have known, now that I think back on it. But everything was always like a movie to Josie. My mother always said she could cry anytime she wanted to. Josie had changed in the last few days, a straightening of her whole body that made her seem more elegant and adult than she ever had before, but this part of her would never die out. Somehow, I am glad for this.

Daddy glanced back once and our eyes touched. He looked sad, too. But lately he always looked sad.

We left Josie on the porch and sauntered out to the truck, where I struggled to bring the suitcase up to the pickup. Daddy finally had to take it from my hands — one pluck from his big, curled fingers — and place it there. I stood silent as my mother embraced Nell, running her hand around Nell's back in a perfect circle.

"You call me and I'll be there, sister," Mom said. It was clear they had already discussed this at length. "You know you don't have to do this by yourself."

Nell nodded, her eyes glassy. "I will. I promise."

Then here came Edie, scampering across the yard with her Chuck Taylors plomping on the dry grass. Nell leaned down to hug her.

"Good old Edie, the best girl I ever knew," Nell said in a singsong voice, almost like a verse from the Beatles, then kissed her on the forehead. "I'll see you on the flip side, hell-cat. Don't take any crap off the boys."

"I won't," Edie said, her face fierce with understanding and remorse. My mother put her hand on Edie's back and led her away. I suppose Mom couldn't bear to watch the truck leave, afraid she might not be called to Nell's bedside once she was needed. Daddy got into the truck but didn't start it. He accepted that Nell had to tell me good-bye properly.

My anger had built by this time, since it was becoming more and more clear that Nell was actually going to leave. I couldn't believe her gall.

"But *why* do you have to leave?" I said. My voice came out scratchy and raw. "Why did you even come if you were going to run off and leave us?"

She gave a little laugh, a simple exhalation of joy or frustration; I couldn't tell which. "I had to come and see you all," she said. "I told you, I was missing home. I was missing the trees."

"So don't leave," I said. I *implored*. "Stay here and let us help you."

"I've got to move on. This is the first time in my life I don't actually want to, but this time I have to, baby." She stuck a knuckle into my belly and smiled down at me. I didn't know that she was going back to DC for the better hospitals there. Or that I would get to go there before long to see her. "You'll understand eventually, Eli the Good."

Even though she had addressed me, it seemed she wasn't even talking to me by this time. She was announcing this to the world, to the leaves. But then she squatted down on cracking knees and she gave me a single kiss on the forehead. I could feel its mark standing on my skin.

She said she loved me, the words a solid thing that drifted out on the air so that I could see their letters against the darkening sky. All around me the sound of the cicadas rose up. "Keep watching; watch everything," she said.

I stood for a long time in the dirt driveway, long after Daddy's truck had passed from my view. And then I was aware of my mother standing behind me. She put her hands on my shoulders. "Come on in. We'll have whatever you want for supper."

"I'd like some Manwich," I said, and she laughed a little in the back of her throat and said this would be okay. I walked around to the back porch with her, leaning into her side.

My mother's red notebook was lying on the table, so I took my Prince Albert cigar box of pencils and crayons out of my room and came back to the kitchen to draw. Josie was in her room, playing her Mamas and Papas record that Nell had given to her, and this sound drifted down the hall and joined us. "Dream a Little Dream of Me." Mom hummed along as she fried the hamburger. I was surprised by her happiness in the wake of Nell leaving, but maybe she was just trying to make things cheerful for me.

"I always loved this song," Mom said. She had turned toward me and she leaned on the counter, her hands resting on its edge. She closed her eyes on the word *love,* like someone savoring a particularly good taste. Then she swayed toward me and held out her hand. "We ought to dance, Eli. It's been a while."

"I don't feel like it," I said, and barely glanced up from my coloring. I was drawing our house in winter. Winter seemed to have not happened in ages. This summer had been the longest one of my life. I had added a chimney with a curl of smoke even though we didn't have a fireplace, and a snowman on the front yard.

I kept coloring a bit before I realized that she was still

standing there with her hand out. But when I looked up at her, she seemed to be someone else, as if her body had been left behind, her feet planted as if nailed to the kitchen floor, while she herself floated somewhere out over the hills, dipping and occasionally rolling over on the air as she flew in the evening sky. She was staring at me.

"Mom?" I said, and her eyes snapped into focus.

"Eli, don't you know that I'd die for you?" she said. She put her hand on the back of my chair and leaned down to where I was turned to face her, looking me in the eye.

"No," I said. Her question seemed like the kind that needed answering properly.

"Well, you should know that. I would. I'd kill for you. You and Josie are my world. You do know that, don't you?"

I gave one quick nod. I did believe her, instantly. But I had been waiting to hear this said to me, proven to me, for a very long time. I turned back to my coloring. I filled each of our windows with yellow light. She turned on one heel and walked back to the stove, where she flipped the sizzling hamburger. Down the hall, Josie put the needle on the song once more, then again, and again, and we listened to it four more times. On the last play, my mother started dancing by herself at the stove, closing her eyes and moving around on the linoleum with one hand flat against her belly, the other out in the air as if holding on to someone. I went to the refrigerator and attached my winter picture with four plastic fruit magnets. And then I joined her.

PART FOUR

The End of Summer

*For nowadays the world is lit
by lightning.*

— Tennessee Williams,
The Glass Menagerie

And so now I am grown. I stand on the ridge above our house, and little has changed to the naked eye. My mother and Stella still share a garden patch. The clothesline is still there, the screen porch. The snowball bush that held me and Edie like a flowery womb. The river that will never change, going about its business as usual, but filled with fewer swimmers now. The road has been widened and black-topped. The bicycles are showy and have painted flames on their bars. And the children don't ride as much as they once did. I doubt there are any silent little boys who sit in the roots of this beech tree anymore. The woods is a lost place to them all, a fact that grieves me.

I am also grieved that my own child has not known this place as I did. She is only ten — the same age I was during the summer of 1976 — but all the years of her life she has known nothing but New York City, a noble place in its own right but one that doesn't possess trees half so noble as the ones of my childhood. And now she is a child living through a war. Perhaps she is not fully aware of this yet, but a part of her is. She eyes gleaming airplanes with suspicion. The little plastic army men she likes to play with are colored a yellowish brown instead of the green ones I always had. The cheap tanks that come in the packs are camouflaged for the desert instead of the jungle. Maybe she doesn't remember what it was like to be evacuated from our apartment on Fourteenth Street or the way the ash piled up and people wore masks when they walked the streets and how my parents begged me to come home and how I wouldn't because that would have felt like defeat to me. But a part of her knows this. It has become a part of her history. I have raised my daughter in the city that knows this new war all too well, the city that saw pumping towers of smoke drifting out over the harbor for three days, smoke that is now replaced by twin beams of blue light when the anniversary of tragedy rolls around. This is my daughter's history now.

I have come home to Refuge for a new part of that history. Daddy has passed away.

He has died of a heart attack. Not suicide, not the effects of Agent Orange, nothing like that. But my mother still believes the war killed him. "All that in his mind," she said when I first saw her. "It was too much for his heart." I don't know whether this is true, but I know that he carried the war around all the time. In his heart, surely. But also in his back, in his feet. The war was always there, in the lines of his face, in his voice, in everything. War seeped in and never let go.

When Josie called and told me that our father was dead, I was alone in my apartment in New York City. After I told her I'd be home and said good-bye, I dropped the phone to the floor. I didn't really notice when it crashed onto the tile and broke, the batteries skittering across the room. I stood at my bedroom window, looking out onto the brick wall that had been my view for the past ten years. There was nothing but the brick. But just over that wall was the purpling sky above the harbor, where night was fixing to spread tight and black. The gloaming.

The next thing I knew, we were on the quiet train: me, my daughter, and Nell. The train dropped below the harbor — all that churning, gray water — and the sounds became heightened, every clank and screech of metal, every long, hollow expanse of darkness made audible. Then we were out again, the train surging forward one car at a time until it gained momentum again, and before I even realized it, we were at the airport and then on the plane. The windows were pocked by specks of rain that tapped like gravels against the glass. The beads of water wouldn't allow me to see out as we left New York on that stormy night of high summer.

I was glad; I didn't want to see.

As the plane took off, I held my daughter's little hand and closed my eyes for a short prayer, as I always did when I flew. This time, though, I didn't open them for a long while, drifting off into some grievous place between sleep and awareness.

I haven't been comfortable flying since 2001, when the world shifted and became off-kilter, blurring everything. But I was less terrified this time. My mind was too full of my father and of the summer I first truly knew him, back when I first saw the war inching its way beneath his skin, behind his eyes.

And I also saw that a person never does know anything, really, until they have lost someone they love completely.

When I was a child, I had thought that life was as simple as black and white. But all at once, sitting on that plane, I knew that we are a people forever caught up in grayness.

Despite the circumstances, I am glad to be home.

I will see Edie for the first time in more than two years, back when she came to New York and I realized that I had never really gotten over her existence. We had walked the streets of Manhattan for hours while she hugged herself against the cold, pulling her topcoat tightly about herself and studying all the faces we passed, saying how beautiful everyone was here. I had shown her all the missing persons posters that still hung in the windows of Saint Vincent's Hospital. Many of them already had yellowed or faded from only a year of sunlight.

"They're letting them age naturally," Edie had said, putting her finger on the window. "That seems right."

We had ridden out to Ellis Island together on the coldest day of the year, and I had given her my gloves because she hadn't brought any. For a brief moment when we passed the Statue of Liberty, she had looked at my face too long, her eyes more revealing than she intended. We stood that way a minute, and then she leaned on the metal railing and peered back out at the harbor, the silence an understood thing between us. We were freezing, but the sky and the water were both gray and beautiful, and all I kept thinking was that she was the only person who had ever truly known me, who could read my mind.

We have not seen each other since then.

I haven't brought my daughter's mother because our marriage is over. It only lasted three years, because my wife and I didn't know each other at all. I am blessed that it ended on good terms. We are clichés, the divorced parents who are able to get along. We both attend Shelby's birthday parties, live within walking distance of each other, talk the way we did when we first met at Vanderbilt. I have even had lunch with her new boyfriend, a lawyer from California who seems like a good man, despite being slightly annoying.

When I see Edie this time, I will see her with new eyes. Who knows what all will happen, for life too has a way of taking up residence, of doing its own thing. I feel as if Edie is already down there at the house, too. Perhaps she is sitting on the screen porch, and any second she will rise and sway out to the steps she knows better than her own, peer up at the woods with her eyes trying to find me among the leaves that are glowing green with the remnants of the heavy rain. A late-summer rain makes the woods turn electric, lighting up the leaves and setting the secret world of the woods into activity. After a good rain, the ants are out and about, salvaging their goods. Deer and foxes venture out to drink from the little freshets that burst out of the mountain. As I look down at the house, the woods are alive with dripping music all around me.

I'm betting that Nell is down there on the screen porch, but no longer smoking. Just like she promised, Nell did not die at the end of that summer. She lost both her breasts to a surgeon's knife, but she lived. She chose life and went on living, raising all manners of hell during the last presidential election, marching in the pink-ribboned protest for better research. We have flown from New York together, taken the long quiet ride from the airport together, entertained by my daughter. I can't see her from up here, but I know she is there. I imagine she is reading one of her thick books and slowly trying to forgive herself for anything that was left unsaid between her and my father.

My mother is down there, too, most likely with Shelby on her lap. Or maybe leaning on her elbow beside Shelby as she helps her draw a picture. She was inconsolable until Shelby came, and my daughter has stuck close by ever since, sensing that if she moves too far away, her grandmother will become a ghost of herself again, a grief-stricken shell that Shelby does not recognize.

And I know that Josie is not far either, probably somewhere down there at the house complaining about something. She never left Refuge. Both she and Edie made the choice to stay, the choice I have considered many times over the years. Josie finally found a man whom she couldn't control and married him and now they live out on the lake in a glass-fronted house. He plays the guitar for her while she lies back and relaxes after a long day of teaching history at the high school.

Josie has remained friends with Charles Asher, and I'm glad for this. He is a part of our family more than he would have been had he become my brother-in-law. He never married, maybe because he never completely got over Josie, but maybe because he's not the marrying kind. I've never asked him, and I figure when he's ready for me to know, he'll tell me. He runs his father's hardware store and held off as long as he could before closing down the drive-in. He is still a good man, one of the best I have ever known, and the last person I know who writes me long, handwritten letters instead of e-mails. It is strange to know that my sister's teenage boy-friend has become my closest male friend in our adulthood. He had stayed close to my father also, and has been with my mother ever since it happened, so he is down there, too.

So everyone I love the most is in that house of mourn-ing. And the gloaming is moving around me, and I stand by this beech tree and prepare for my father's funeral. The loss of him is too much to bear, and I have come to my old beech tree to seek solace. I was always able to find it here.

I keep turning over in my mind all the things I should have said to my father, all the little moments of connection I let pass by. I am thinking of the night — my thirtieth birthday — he sat down and talked for hours about Vietnam, his blunt-tipped fingers pointing out details in the photographs. I wonder if he knew how much I respected him.

I think of the day Nell and I marched in the silent pro-test against this new war. The whole time, I was wondering what my father would think if he saw us on the news, if he found out that I was a war protester now. If he had men-tioned it to me, I would have told him that I marched for him, for all of us. To make sure the protest was done with balance, to show that we had all learned a lesson about speaking out with compassion for everyone involved. As we walked hand in hand down Seventh Avenue, I saw my father's face in the windows of each building we passed, smelled home in the breeze that billowed across the avenue from the Hudson.

My whole life I have been haunted not only by what my father went through in Vietnam, but also by what he went through when he returned. I feel the need to honor him, and the best way to do that is by standing up for what I believe in, just as he did.

I try, and fail, to push away the guilt of having left Refuge, thinking of how much more time I could have had with him if I had only stayed here. Why I left, I don't know. I have never found a place of more beautiful night sounds, have never found a place where I so completely belonged despite being different. I recall Nell saying to me that she came back to see all of us that summer but also came back to see the trees, that you never forget the trees of your childhood, and that—more important—they never forget you. She was right.

The beech tree says its old, true mantra: *I am here.* And this is a balm. But for the first time, the tree does more. Because it comforts me by reminding me of the last day of that summer back in 1976, when Daddy found me in this place I had thought was my own secret place, not knowing that it was his, too.

. . .

I sat in the roots of the beech, leaning back against the trunk, letting its coolness sink into my skin. No matter how hot the air, the tree was always cool, as if pulling up the dampness its roots tapped into far below the earth. This beech was solid, unmovable.

That's where I chose to spend my last hours of true summer, the day before school started back. After Nell had gone, after Edie and I had played in the creek until our feet were wrinkled from the water, after I had situated my notebook paper into my new three-ring binder and held my pencils up to my face to draw in their school scent, I had climbed the ridge up to my tree.

I had brought along my composition book and was trying to write down anything about this summer that I hadn't already gotten on paper. I sat studying about everything that had happened in the past three months, and before I knew it, I curled up there in that familiar place with the call of jays above me and went to sleep. There was no better place to nap than there, no place where the world smelled so new and safe. My mother would have fainted if she had known I liked to sleep there, where snakes crawled on the ridge. I had seen them myself. But I never thought about the snakes much. I figured if I didn't bother them, they'd leave me alone, too. Apparently I was right, since I had never had a waking encounter with one. Most things are like that: just trying to get by in the world until you mess with them.

I lay my head in the crook of one of the roots and imagined the little fox — grown now, by summer's end — watching me, considering the way we had both changed. Mine was a bluish-gray sleep. For a time I was still conscious of the birdcall over me like a murmuring quilt, the way the wind breathed through the beech leaves, the little cracks and pops that a forest gives off if you listen closely enough. But then I was plunged into a thick, black sleep.

That's how I was when my father approached, going for his evening walk.

I wonder how he saw me in that moment when he came up the ridge to the secret tree he had known all of his life, ever since he was a boy. Was he surprised that I had made this my secret place, too? Did he wonder how we had gone so long without crossing paths here, since he had visited the beech often since returning from Vietnam?

He spied on me sleeping, encircled by tree roots, an ant — undetected by me — crawling across my forehead. I like to think that he whispered thanks for me, for this place that he had missed so much when he was gone overseas. I hope he said a little prayer to the woods. And I bet he squatted there near me and watched me sleep for a time, occasionally laughing in the back of his throat at how much I reminded him of himself. I think that he probably found my composition book lying there where it had slid from my lap. Perhaps he started to open it, but glancing at the writing on the front — *The Private Thoughts of Eli Book* — he thought better of it, and pulled his hand away as if it had gotten too close to an open flame.

But when the sky turned crimson at the horizon and the gloaming began to tick closer and closer, he finally reached out and brushed away the ant and ran his hand over the top of my head. "Wake up, buddy," he whispered. "Wake up."

I didn't say anything when I sat up, amazed that he had found my secret place but also realizing in that moment that perhaps this beech tree had been the same one he had spoken of in his letters. Maybe he had been talking about another tree, but I like to think that we had shared this hiding place, that it joined us.

"Hey," he said, quiet, as if afraid of disturbing the oncoming dusk.

"Is it time for supper?"

He nodded and squatted down. Looked at the forest floor and then studied the sky, took his time in looking at the swaying branches of the beech, the trembling leaves. He was working something around in his mind. I could tell.

I sat on my haunches, too, dusting off my face, where tiny pieces of wood and bits of moss clung to my cheek. I ran my fingers through my hair and discovered two ants.

"There's no other place I'd rather be than right here," he said, and his face smoothed out, released the worry and hurt he had carried there for the last few weeks. Then he turned to me. "Everything's going to be all right, Eli," he said. His eyes stayed on mine. "I promise you that."

I believed him. Somehow, I knew that everything *would* be all right, and a fist of grief and worry uncurled in my stomach, releasing itself. There was certainty in his words, but also in the curve of his shoulders, in his face. Daddy got up, dusted off the back of his work pants, and put his hand out to help me up. We were silent as we moved down the old path. I held his hand and we eased back down to the house where supper was waiting, where my mother would be standing on the back step waiting for us, where Josie would sweep her black hair out of her eyes to smile at us when we sat at the table, where the world shimmered and leveled, ripe with possibility.

ACKNOWLEDGMENTS

I am indebted to so many good friends and family members who helped to make this book possible. I wish I could name them all, but chief among them were Pamela Duncan, Paul Hiers, Jason Howard, Denton Loving, Sylvia Lynch, and Neela Vaswani, all of whom read the book in its earliest stages. Jason Howard gave me the poem "I Think Continually of Those Who Were Truly Great" by Stephen Spender, which inspired the title of this book. I hope you will look it up. Neela Vaswani taught me so much about everything I can never repay her. One of my favorite things about this book is the way it looks at friendship; everyone in this paragraph is a true example of that. I don't know what I'd do without them.

Larry Brown was the first person to read the first chapter of this book and encouraged me to keep writing. I miss you, bro. Clint McCown published the short story "1976" that was the impetus for this novel, so he was the first one to love the Book Family; thank you. Stephanie Tittle answered botanical questions with wit and grace. Kirby Gann played the guitar one night and inspired a scene. Lee Smith talked me through the hard times, and that's just one more of the many, many things to thank her for. Lisa Parker's poetry and spirit were both inspirations. I thank her for showing me the great beating heart of New York City. Glenn Cornett devoted an afternoon to me, graciously and patiently answering all of my questions about post-traumatic stress disorder. My sister, Eleshia Sloan, is a constant light in my life.

A special thanks to my people at Lincoln Memorial University, Spalding University, and the Hindman Settlement School. Keith Semmel and Marianne Worthington gave me ABBA albums and answered questions about the Beatles (and are pretty great friends to boot). My agent, Joy Harris, never lost faith in this character or this book. I thank her and Adam Reed for their hard work. Thanks to Gigi Amateau for her part in all of this. And special thanks to Karen Lotz and Nicole Raymond, who understood and loved Eli as I did. They, like everyone at Candlewick Press, worked hard on this novel, and I owe them.

My daughters, Cheyenne and Olivia, were instrumental in allowing me to go back in time and remember the wonder and sadness a child possesses. I thank them for taking photographs that informed my writing, for laughter that kept me going, and for being the strong, beautiful people they are. I'm so glad they exist.

Thanks to all of the above. In this life, I have loved them all.

DATE DUE

JUN 04			
JAN 5 '77			
MAY 5			
OCT 27			
			5.7